A HUSBAND'S KISS

"I believe I owe you an apology, Victoria."

She offered no comment, merely sat quietly waiting for him to continue. There was no softening of the expression on her pretty face.

His voice dropped lower, taking on a soft, silky quality. "I should have given you a chance to explain about having run your family estate and about your legacy. Instead I was rude and overbearing."

Still the lady sat staring at him, making no attempt to end the animosity between them. Realizing he wanted to do more than give her empty words, he came to stand beside her. There as a slight quiver to her full lips as he drew near, making her look utterly feminine and defenseless. He took her hand, drawing her to her feet. He was filled with the need to kiss away her fear about him, the marriage, or both. Then the delicate scent of roses filled his senses and he struggled to resist the urge to take complete possession of his wife at that very moment. He reminded himself she was young and innocent. He had to take his time to woo this delectable creature to his bed. With that in mind, he cupped her chin with his hands.

"Forgive me for failing to tell you that you are beautifully enchanting, my dear." Kit's mouth then covered hers hungrily. Her tentative response was so innocent and sweet, she stirred his desire as never before. . . .

Books by Lynn Collum

A GAME OF CHANCE

ELIZABETH AND THE MAJOR

THE SPY'S BRIDE

Published by Zebra Books

THE SPY'S
BRIDE

LYNN COLLUM

Zebra Books
Kensington Publishing Corp.

http://www.zebrabooks.com

For my best friend and sister, Donna Collum.
Thanks for all your love and support.

ZEBRA BOOKS are published by

Kensington Publishing Corp.
850 Third Avenue
New York, NY 10022

First Printing: January, 1999
10 9 8 7 6 5 4 3 2 1

Printed in the United States of America

PROLOGUE

Portugal—December, 1810

A blanket of darkness edged upward in the eastern sky as a tall man made his way along the narrow winding streets of Salamanca. His gait was a bit unsteady, as if he'd drunk too deeply of the fine Portuguese wine, but he attracted no undue attention in the nearly empty streets. He was dressed as sedately as any young Portuguese gentleman of good birth. His only flaw was his height. A black beaver hat was pulled low, leaving his eyes obscured in shadow by the fading daylight. A dust-coated black cape swirled about his ankles, billowing as he walked.

He looked back over his shoulder to make certain no one was following. Then he stopped along the row of faded whitewashed buildings at a weathered door with a faint image of a seven etched into the stone.

A soft tap brought an old Portuguese woman to

the door. She peered out into the near darkness, a hint of fear in her ebony eyes.

"Padre Cortes?" the man hoarsely inquired, using the name the locals called the priest.

She nodded her black-scarfed head and gestured the visitor to enter. *"Sim, ele está aqui."*

The gentleman removed his hat and ducked his head to pass through the low doorway. He entered a small dank room smelling of smoke, sausage and dirt. A lone candle burned at an ancient wooden table surrounded by chairs, the only pieces of furniture in the room. A fire blazed in the fireplace, scarcely taking the chill from the humble chamber.

The old woman pulled out one of the crudely made chairs and pointed for him to be seated. She smiled and nodded her head while she poured wine into an earthen pottery cup which she extended to him. After he took the offering, she exited through a door on the far side of the room.

Kit tossed down the wine in one gulp, then collapsed into the chair to await the padre or whoever might come in his stead. He reached into his jacket and pulled out a leather-bound document, tossing it on the table beside his hat. He drew back the cape to inspect the saber wound. It was deep. Blood still oozed from the makeshift bandage he'd applied hours ago.

The door through which the old woman had disappeared opened, and a man, dressed in black robes with a large silver cross around his neck, stepped into the room. He paused and eyed the young man at the table before coming forward. He lifted the fabric of the dark green jacket to inspect the bound wound.

In English, but with a marked Irish accent, the father said, "Christopher, would you be tryin' to get yourself killed with all your gallivantin' round in the mountains.''

The young man shook his head. "Not I, Dr. Curtis. I'm just a Portuguese gentleman going about my business who was waylaid by brigands.''

Dr. Patrick Curtis was a professor of astronomy and theology at the Irish Catholic University of Salamanca. It was a puzzle to Kit, that with the long history of bad blood with Ireland, the father willingly worked for the British, but he never questioned the old man as to his reasons.

The priest turned, calling the woman in Portuguese to bring water and bandages. He looked back at Kit, shaking his head. "Don't be takin' the French for fools, laddie. 'Tis lookin' for *le Fantôme Anglais,'* they are. Your mother may be Portuguese, but you're as proper an English viscount as ever I did see, no matter you speakin' the language like a local. Now you should be takin' off that coat and shirt so Maria can do with it what she can before mornin'.''

"No, Doctor, first read the dispatch I captured. You will see it's imperative you send a message to Don Julian Sanchez, at once.'' Kit knew gold was being offered for the English Phantom but there was little he could do about the price on his head. It was too important that the Spanish *guerilla* leader learn there was a highly placed traitor among his band of men. It had been Kit's task to find the French informer and by a stroke of good luck the man's name was in the captured dispatch on the table.

The priest frowned, picking up the bound leather packet. "Wellington has all manner of officers capturin' dispatches. You're too valuable to your government to be riskin' your life on such matters. Don't you know.'' Untying the leather strap, the old man quickly read the French message. His gaze lifted to meet Kit's, a troubled expression on his face. " 'Tis right you are, laddie. This is important. I'll return in a moment."

While Kit waited for Dr. Curtis to return, the old woman cleaned and dressed his wound. Before leaving the room, she gave him a rough homespun wool shirt to wear, telling him she would have his own ready by morning.

The priest returned. "Maria is preparin' a bed where you might sleep. What are you plannin' come mornin'?"

"My mission is complete. I return to Lisbon then back to England."

"Then may God go with you, my son." Dr. Curtis made the sign of the cross, then shook Kit's hand. "Until we meet again, Christopher." The old man went to the outer door. He listened first, then quickly opened the door, shutting it almost as fast after he'd passed through.

Kit knew the priest wasn't being overly cautious. There was always someone willing to pay for information about unusual activities. Maria came in and led him to a small airless room where he lay down upon a cot with a musty wool blanket. He was too tired to care about the amenities. It would be good to get home to England, but he hoped no new catastrophe awaited him

CHAPTER ONE

England, January 1811

"There is no other solution. You *must* marry Lady Victoria." Orson Woodley, the eighth Earl of Stonebridge leaned back and glared down the long table at his son who sat playing with his spoon, his strawberry trifle uneaten. There was a vacant look in the boy's pale blue eyes.

At the opposite end of the table, a faded blonde took exception to her husband's declaration. Normally the timidest of creatures, the countess, a frail, anxious female, became quite the lioness when her son's future was so much in jeopardy. "You would tie your only son to his hoydenish cousin. Why, she is the most spoiled, managing female it has ever been my misfortune to meet. Has she not tried to insinuate herself into estate matters since you've taken up the reins at Stoneleigh? No doubt when married, she will presume that she and not Giles should run the estate, since she did so while her father was ill."

The earl's face grew red as he turned his stony gaze on his wife. "No one but I shall run this estate for a good many years, madam. I believe you are quite finished with your dinner. Retire to the drawing room and allow my son and I to discuss this matter in private."

Vera Woodley trembled under her husband's scrutiny. As much as she wished to protect Giles, she dared not defy Orson's command. She rose as a footman stepped forward and drew back her chair. With handkerchief to stifle her sniffles, the countess hurried from the dining room.

Lord Stonebridge again turned to his son who had yet to give the slightest response to the matter under discussion. The boy sat there with a vacant expression on his round face, no doubt his head in the clouds, as if he hadn't a care in the world. Fury built in the father, causing him to roar at his only offspring. "Are you listening to me, you nodcock?"

The young man started then sat a bit straighter. "What say, Father? Going to a cockfight?"

"I said you must marry Lady Victoria at once."

"Marry my cousin! But she . . . she . . ." Lord Giles Woodley sat up and looked about him frantically as he took his father's meaning.

"I have only just discovered the girl will inherit fifty thousand pounds on her marriage and this estate is virtually penniless." The earl had learned of the mysterious stranger from London who'd visited his niece after his brother's death. The fellow had been traced to a solicitor in Lombard Street and the earl had spent a pretty penny bribing a clerk to know the nature of the business with the girl.

Giles ran trembling fingers through his long golden curls, causing his father to frown. The younger Woodley thought himself a poet, to his father's disgust, and dressed like a raffish vagabond as suited his image of a poet, wearing his hair unfashionably long and unbound, eschewing a cravat for a black scarf knotted at his throat and leaving half the buttons on his waistcoat undone.

"I don't think she likes me above half. Besides, she is a redhead, a most unfashionable color. Not likely to get any suitable poems about red hair. I'd be—"

The earl slammed his hand on the table, causing the footman filling the wineglasses to jump. "I don't care if she has a head like Medusa, we must have that money. Do I make myself clear? You leave for London in the morning to secure a Special License."

Orson Woodley, tall and well built for his forty-five years, had the nature of a brute. As the footman came to remove the untouched dish in front of him, the earl waved him away. "Be gone you fool."

Theo, five years a servant at the manor, cast one pitying glance at Lord Giles, who'd pulled out a rumpled piece of paper and pencil to write. His lordship was right, the boy was a fool, the footman thought as he left the room for the kitchens, full of news.

Lord Stonebridge noticed his son was occupied scribbling something down. "What the devil are you doing?"

Giles looked up, eyes sparkling. "Head of Medusa, you said. Gave me a splendid notion for a sonnet."

The young man again bowed his head to compose his opus, completely unaware that his father had risen and come round the table. With lightning swiftness, he tore the paper from Giles's hand, glared at the writing, then stepped to the fireplace and tossed it in.

"Enough of your foolish scribblings. Are you going to do as I wish?" His voice quavered his ire was so great.

The young man was suddenly brought out of his musings by his parent's tone. Having always been a disappointment to his father, Giles wondered if this marriage might at last allow him to bask in that gentleman's approval. After all, it wasn't as though he would have to live with his cousin as a husband. The thought made him shudder. He knew there were men who could handle a woman who was fearless, waspish and managing, but not he. What he longed for was a gentle Venus or a beautiful Aphrodite. Trouble was, he depended on his father's largess.

He bit his lip pensively as his irate parent loomed over him. Giles hadn't known that his cousin was an heiress, not that it would have made her any more tolerable, with her sharp tongue and disdainful ways. But if they had the money, Giles reasoned, he could spend all his time in Town with his friends. The notion suddenly held appeal. "Very well, Father, I leave for London tomorrow to secure the license, as you wish."

Soon the gentlemen fell to discussing the details of the forthcoming nuptials, one with a great deal more enthusiasm than the other. They were unaware that Theo was at that very moment seeking out Betty, Lady Victoria's maid. The information he whispered into that devoted woman's ear caused her to hurry to the west wing.

The young maid knocked sharply on the door, then entered to find her mistress seated at her writing desk, quill in hand. The young lady had pleaded a headache to get out of dining with her uncle and his wife, but Betty was certain that Lady Victoria had not been ill a day in her life. "Oh, my lady, there be evil doin's afoot."

Lady Victoria Woodley looked up from the letter she was penning to her cousin Charles in Lisbon. She had been debating what to tell her childhood companion about the new earl, his faded wife, and their foolish son when her maid entered. She didn't wish to pour out all her fears about Uncle Orson to Charles.

Victoria laid down her quill and rose. Dressed in black to honour her parent's memory, she could not mourn his release from his paralyzed body. Her red hair seemed all the brighter against the dark hued wool. Its flame colour was a bane to her, red curls never being in fashion, but she had long ago put aside thoughts of cutting a dash in Society or even marriage. She knew little of matrimony, only what she'd experienced from observing her parent's warring match, but it had given her little taste for the holy estate.

A gift from beyond the grave now made it possible for her to chose her own path. Scarcely a month ago she'd learned of the legacy she was to inherit from her maternal grandfather's estate, long thought squandered on the green baize by her father. But the funds had been out of his reach due to a secret codicil in the older man's will. With her unexpected inheritance she might purchase an estate which would be her very own and not to be lost by an entail, as Stoneleigh had been.

As her maid drew near, Victoria noted that the girl's cheeks were excessively flushed. "Betty, what foolishness is this? Evil at Stoneleigh Manor. You haven't been letting Anna read to you from those dreadful Minerva Press novels again?''

The girl grabbed her mistress's hands. '' 'Tis nothin' to do with silly stories about Eye-talian counts, but danger for you, my lady.''

Victoria looked closely at her servant's face. Her heart grew cold. "You have heard something."

"Not I, but Theo. His lordship says you are to inherit a large sum of money and he wants Lord Giles to get it for him. Marriage is the scheme."

The colour drained from Victoria's face. How had Uncle Orson discovered the legacy? She'd been at such pains to keep the information secret as her grandfather intended. She hadn't even written to her cousin Charles news of the change in her circumstances. She drew her hands from Betty's and wrapped her arms about her as a chill ran down her spine.

So she was to be forced into marriage with Giles. No doubt it was the very thing her grandfather had feared. There was nothing like an heiress to bring the fortune hunters to call. While Victoria knew Giles to be a harmless fool, she had no such illusions about Lord Stonebridge. Clever, cruel and without scruple, the gentleman brooked no defiance in his family. Did he mistake her for his simpering wife, or for his spineless son, to be ordered about as if she hadn't plans of her own making? She vowed to herself a wedding would never take place between her and her cousin.

Her hands fell away from her sides as she straightened her back. "I shall never marry Cousin Giles."

Betty frowned. "But how shall you prevent the earl from forcin' that Jack-a-dandy on you. He's your guardian. Gentlemen like his lordship have ways of gettin' what they want. Oh, if only Captain Rydal weren't in Portugal, Lord Stonebridge wouldn't even be thinkin' of such a thing since they share your guardianship.''

"Charles.'' Victoria's face brightened at the mention of her cousin who was with Wellington's army in the Peninsula. Betty was right. The captain would surely protect her and her future inheritance. In truth, as is often the case with relatives one grew up with, they could barely be in one another's company for over five minutes without quarreling over some trivial matter. But her governess had always declared it was that they were too much alike—determined, headstrong and confident.

Victoria wouldn't let a little matter like their spats keep her from asking for her cousin's help. He might be forever criticizing her and reprimanding her, but he was an honourable young man. He wouldn't allow their uncle to force her into this marriage.

She walked to the window, drew aside the green drape, and gazed with unseeing eyes into the January darkness. If only there were time, she would summon Charles home. But he'd been wounded in November while under command of General Blake pursuing Marshal Soult near Granada. He was currently on light duty in Lisbon until his wounds healed.

Time was her enemy. Giles could travel to London and back in a mere four days. She would be married to the vain silly fellow before the captain could be notified of her situation and come to Stoneleigh.

There was only one solution. She must go to the captain. After all, most of the fighting had moved to Spain, had it not? But the very thought of going was so audacious that a slight shudder ran through Victoria. The danger of such an expedition was frightening to think about. Should she risk her life, not to mention her reputation on such an adventure? For a young woman to set out alone for Portsmouth, to board a ship and then disembark on the war-torn soil of the Peninsula was the height of folly.

Shaking her head, she knew the true folly would be to remain, and allow Lord Stonebridge and his son to steal her future. With her usual determination, Victoria dropped the curtain and turned to face Betty. "I shan't be anyone's pawn. I shall go to the Peninsula to Charles."

The little maid's grey eyes grew round. "Have you taken leave of your senses, my lady? You can't be goin' to some heathen land what's at war." The girl paused for a minute, a thoughtful expression coming to her pink-cheeked face. "What am I sayin'? His lordship will have caught you within a day's time. With that hair and fine figure, everyone will remember a lady travelin' without a proper chaperon, for don't be thinkin' I'll follow you into this hare-brained scheme. I've got my mother to support."

Lady Victoria walked to her dressing table to stare at her reflection. Betty was right. Whenever she went into Carlisle, people took notice of her bright curls, no doubt out of pity. They were an unusual hue. Her late governess had likened it to the flames of Satan's fire. As to her figure, God had been overgenerous with the blessing of her bosom.

With a defiant toss of her head, which caused the detested red curls to bounce, she declared, "Then I shall have to manage a way to disguise both features. I tell you, Betty, I *am* going to Portugal."

Lord Christopher Harden, Viscount Ridgecrest, known as Kit to his friends and family, absentmindedly rubbed the healing wound on his left shoulder. He sat before the roaring fire in his library lost in thought. He'd arrived home a little over a week ago, a fever having felled him in Lisbon. As he feared, a new catastrophe awaited him at Harwick. Cook was on the verge of leaving after his mother had ordered the woman to never again set an insipid Yorkshire pudding upon their table.

Mrs. Blaine, being from the West Riding, had taken offense and was packing to depart just as Kit arrived. He'd spent the better part of the week making peace between the two women, convincing each that she, no doubt, was right in her thinking.

With things settled once again into a quieter routine, he'd managed to find the peace to sit before the library fire to inspect the books kept by his bailiff. As he perused the rows of numbers, he knew things had become quite serious for the estate.

Harwick Hall, as his late father had named the rundown property four and a half years ago when he'd purchased the estate, needed Kit's full attention if he were to make it fully livable and more profitable. He'd spent more time on government business than on his own affairs and wasn't certain why he'd taken the job of going deep into Portugal and Spain trying to root out traitors. There was certainly little money or glory involved, besides it being quite dangerous.

Perhaps he'd just been flattered to be requested by the Duke of York to prove his mettle to his country, or maybe he was trying to prove to his estranged grandfather, the Duke of Townsend, that despite a Portuguese mother, Kit was English to his very core.

More likely the true reason had been, that at four and twenty, he just hadn't been ready to settle down to the quiet life of managing an estate. He'd seen

and done a lot over the four years since he'd made
the faithful decision to work for Horse Guards. The
fire for adventure burned less bright with each mission. Only obligation to his country kept him going
now. As long as he was useful, he would help where
he could.

Still, he welcomed the occasional chance to get
away from the brangling women in his household
and the infernal renovations the manor needed. His
father, the late viscount, had purchased the neglected
estate after fleeing from Portugal with his wife and
daughter, hoping to make Harwick profitable again.
Since his father's death nothing seemed to please
either his sister or mother. They managed to quarrel
about the simplest things from what colour to choose
for the curtains, to the size of the slate tiles for the
kitchen floor. Kit had given up on the improvements
to the house in frustration before he'd barely begun.

Now his mother had taken to suggesting he find a
wealthy wife. One who could help him afford the
renovations the house needed as well as make all
those annoying decisions. The one thing Kit was certain about was he didn't need another woman to
further complicate his life.

With a sigh, he tenderly kneaded the wound, sink-
ing deeper into his dark mood. It seemed as if his
father's death had thrown a pall over the entire family
from which they hadn't been able to escape. No doubt
it had been one of life's ironies that Martin Harden,
who'd vowed never to return to England after quarreling with his father, had been forced to sell his wine
exporting business in Oporto and flee the invading
French soldiers. Kit's father died at Harwick a month
later of a lung inflammation.

A knock sounded on the door, causing Kit to drop

his hand away from the wound. Only Jose, his late father's manservant, knew where the viscount went on his long trips from home. His mother and sister thought he kept rooms in London for the work he did at Horse Guards, not donning disguises and mixing with *guerrillas* who fought the French.

An ancient, slatternly servant stepped into the room. "My lord, yer mother wishes to see ye in the rear parlor at yer convenience."

"Thank you, Martha."

The maid shuffled away as Kit lifted the ledger he'd been perusing and laid it on the table. He rose smoothing the fabric on the sleeve of his wounded arm.

With a resigned sigh, he went to see what his mother wanted. Entering the drawing room, he crossed to join his mother and sister. *"Bom dia, Mamãe. Bom dia,* Isabel."

Also speaking Portuguese, Luisa, the dowager Lady Ridgecrest, looked up from her tambour, a quarrelsome tone in her voice. "Kit, Martha says there is to be no more coal for the fireplace. I shall catch my death of cold without proper heat in this miserable English weather."

"Coal is expensive, and there is wood in abundance on the estate. You shall not be left to freeze, *Mamãe.*" The viscount walked to the fireplace and placed another log on the grate then stood and propped his good arm on the mantelpiece before realizing it hadn't been dusted this week. He lifted his elbow and the dark blue coat came away with a line of grime on his sleeve.

He knew that the Portuguese standard of cleanliness differed greatly from the English. It came from having little or no glass in the windows of the terraced homes. Open doors and shutters were common during the day to allow the light in. One got used to the dust and dirt which coated nearly every surface. But having spent the better part of the last ten years in England, first in school and then in Town, Kit found his mother's casual acceptance of the dirt difficult to fathom. Her perpetual excuse was that the house was still under repair, so he had only himself to blame. With a sigh, he brushed the dust from his sleeve.

Miss Isabel Harden pulled the black woolen shawl higher on her plump shoulders. Her raven black hair was parted in the middle and pulled to a tight bun at the nape of her neck, black Spanish combs holding the hair in place. "Fire is fire, *Mamãe*, it can make little difference whether it is wood or coal. Besides, we never used coal at Grande Poleiro."

Kit's sister sighed for her lost home in the hills above the Duoro River, then went back to the novel she was reading. It was a pastime her mother deplored, saying it filled Isabel's head with foolish notions, but Miss Harden complained that it was her only entertainment on the remote estate, since her mother refused to allow Isabel any hand in matters of household management.

Lady Ridgecrest, feeling particularly quarrelsome after her son's long unexplained absence, launched into a tirade about the state of their lives. "To think that we sit here, nearly in debtors prison, the house still needing work, while your grandfather lavishes money on his horses in York."

"We are hardly so bad off, *Mamãe* and I shall finish the renovations in my own time. As to Grandfather, his fortune is not entailed, and he may do with it whatever he wishes. If I can ever make heads or tails of those ledgers of Anderson's, I might determine

why the profits for the estate were so low last year."
He hoped he'd have time to decipher the books.
He'd received a message from Lord Carew two days
before to expect a courier with new orders.

"You would do better to spend your time looking
for a rich wife, than to be always at your business in
London for there seems to be little profit in what you
do." Lady Ridgecrest grimaced up at her son.

"I am no fortune hunter, *Mamãe*. A wife will have
to wait until I get my affairs more in order. I could
never bring a bride here until there were major
repairs to the house." Even longer if Kit had his way.

Isabel, hearing the mention of one of her favorite
subjects, piped, "Next time you go to London, can
Mamãe and I not come up to Town with you? You
have said we might go one of these times."

This was an argument Kit had already had with his
sister on more than one occasion. "I am *not* going
to parties when I am again in London and I have
only rooms, not a proper house. I promise I shall
do my best to arrange a Season for you next year."
Wellington seemed to be getting the upper hand. Kit
felt certain that he wouldn't be needed much longer.

"Always next year." Isabel's hand, which had been
resting on a table which held a bowl of nuts, came
up to cover her trembling mouth.

Lady Ridgecrest sat forward. "Did you eat a walnut,
Isabel Harden?"

Defiantly the young lady openly tossed another
piece into her mouth. "So I did, *Mamãe,* but what
does it matter if I am big as a house if no one is to
see me."

Kit frowned at his mother. He could not convince
the lady that Isabel would never be petite. Standing
nearly as tall as himself, she was a large woman with

a full figure, not slight and delicate like their mother. True, she was a bit larger than she should be, but her countenance was pleasing when it wasn't puckered into a frown over her mother's badgering. Of late he noted the more his mother plagued her the more she seemed to eat.

"*Mamãe,* you worry far too much about matters of little import. Isabel, why must you always provoke an—"

The front knocker sounded, interrupting what Kit had been about to say to his sister. He suspected he knew who their visitor was, and the news he brought would cause Kit's mother to forget his sister's weight and Isabel her trip to London. He walked to the door of the small drawing room, uncertain if the unreliable Martha would respond. It was a mystery to him that his mother always managed to quarrel with the servants. In four short years they'd lost nearly every decent maid or footman hired, always leaving them short-handed.

But to Kit's amazement, within minutes the old woman, the lone servant, besides Cook, who remained under his mother's haphazard housekeeping, arrived to announce Major Edward Cooper.

Lady Ridgecrest and Isabel looked at Kit with accusing eyes, knowing the soldier would take Kit away with him. The gentleman in red tunic with cream facings took several wobbly steps into the small room, then fell flat on his face, eddies of dust swirling up around him as he landed on the worn Aubusson carpet.

Kit helped the major rise, hearing his mother muttering in Portuguese, "*This* is one of Wellington's officers." Then she clicked her tongue, adding, "Oh, my dear Portugal is lost."

Once the soldier was fully upright, he politely greeted his hostess as if nothing untoward had occurred. Kit and his family, switching to English for that gentleman's benefit, returned his greeting.

The officer was a man of indeterminate age, for the sun had prematurely weathered his freckled skin. There was no grey in his brown hair, but his cheerful brown eyes were framed by radiating lines.

"Ladies, your servant. Kit, you are looking fit after—"

"Edward," the viscount interrupted fearful that, given the major's cup shot condition, he might be indiscreet. "I was expecting you this morning."

The soldier gave his friend a wry smile. "Frightfully cold outside, Kit. Still recovering from my wound from Bussaco. Stopped at the Speckled Goose for a tankard of their best home brew."

Kit suspected more than one tankard of the inn's fine ale had crossed the major's lips. He quickly made his excuses to the ladies and led the major to his library. The gentleman gave Kit a set of sealed orders, which he placed in his desk drawer unread. He questioned Major Cooper about the news from Horse Guards.

By the time Edward finished telling what he knew of Soult moving north into the Estremadura Provence of Spain, he'd sobered considerably and apologized profusely. Martha came in to light the candles, and the gentlemen had to retire to change for dinner. The orders remained unread. Kit knew generally what they would say: go to Portugal. Only the specifics would be outlined and that at least could wait.

After they'd dined, and his mother, sister and the major were all abed, Kit broke the seal and read the dispatch. The mission was urgent. Someone had information to pass to *le Fantôme Anglais* regarding a plot to kill Wellington. Kit drew a deep breath as he saw the name, then continued to read. He was to meet Sir James Marks in the village of Campo Mayor by the fifteenth of next month, not a day later. Folding the orders, he knew he would don a disguise and go to the border town which now lay on the edge of enemy territory. But this time it was a matter of life and death for the man who was Britain's hope for victory. He and Edward *must* leave for Portsmouth early the next morning.

The old carriage pulled to a stop in front of the North Dock of Portsmouth harbor. A plump young man with badly cut brown curls sticking from beneath a wide-brimmed dusty hat climbed down. He thanked the driver who'd given him a ride from the coaching inn. The lad gazed awestruck by the sight of tall ships anchored just off shore, oblivious to the bitter January winter wind reddening his cheeks. He clutched an old leather satchel tightly to his chest and pondered his next move.

To the casual passerby, the young man looked like a well-fed farmer or upper servant, for there was nothing of the fashionable sprig about him. He wore an unfashionable, brown frock coat, atop a dark green waistcoat which was too long for the current mode. He attracted no undue attention, for no one knew that beneath the many layers of clothing was in fact, a Lady of Quality.

Lady Victoria Woodley was well pleased with the disguise that she and Betty had devised. All the while the young maid had been predicting dire consequences for this foolhardy plan. In truth, the weather had been a great ally in helping them transform Victoria into a man. The young lady had cut and dyed her fiery locks to a muddy brown. She wore four pairs of stockings and three pairs of black wool knee breeches found in the attic and needing a pillow to keep them about her slender waist. She'd donned four shirts, three long old-fashioned waistcoats and a heavy wool frock coat. A loosely tied neck cloth covered the collars of the other shirts as well as hiding the slender column of her neck. The multiple layers of clothing had been welcomed on the cold journey south.

It had been a simple enough matter to leave early the morning after Giles's departure. She'd taken the express coach from Carlisle to London, then on to Portsmouth. The journey had taken a scant three days.

Jostled by some passing fishermen, Victoria turned and walked east, all the while admiring the bay before her. Among the great ships anchored were smaller ones, sails unfurled coming home. Low boats with men manning the oars dotted the harbor, going back and forth to the great ships. The random screech of the occasional gull soaring above the dock added to the charm of the sights.

She came to the landing place at the dock, and watched the activity. Long lines of soldiers were being loaded on to flat boats and poled to the waiting ships. It was a stark reminder that her country was at war.

In the far distance she could see the Isle of Wight through the many ship spires, the sails lashed tightly to the yardarms unneeded. Everything was so new, so exciting, she couldn't regret her decision.

Just as that thought entered her head, she was bumped by two passing sailors. They were officers of the British Navy, for she recognized the neat blue jackets with white knee pants. One wore a low-crowned beaver, the other a round hat with gold loop and cockade. A single epaulet adorned his shoulder.

"Out of the way, boy. Don't you know it ain't safe to be lurking round the docks," the one with the epaulet barked.

The midshipman laughed loudly, poking Victoria in the arm and causing her to draw back. "I'm certain the press gang would be pleased with the likes of you, my good fellow."

"That they would DeVane. We'd have this fellow several stone lighter in a month on the *Amethyst.*" The two sailors chuckled as they walked past the object of their torture.

Victoria suddenly lost all her joy in Portsmouth. Looking back over her shoulder to make certain there was no pressman with cudgel to take her, she hurried down the docks looking for a ship on which she could book passage to Lisbon. The sooner she was safely out of England the better for her.

But the matter was not to be that simple. By late afternoon she'd discovered that all the ships that usually sailed to Lisbon were gone, having embarked over several days of that week. Wherever she asked, Victoria was informed that no ships would again sail for at least a week or more depending on the weather.

"But, sir," Victoria made her voice as deep as possible. "Are you telling me that no one sails for Portugal within the next few days?"

"Didn't say that, lad." The dock master looked up from the log he was writing in, giving the plump boy a grin.

Excitement raced through Victoria. "Then there is a way I can get to Lisbon."

"Aye, there be. You take the king's shillin' and you'll be there afore you know it." The man laughed heartily at his own joke.

"Take the king's shilling?" Victoria didn't understand.

"Join the army, you silly bantlin'. I hear the *Avenge,* the *Denmark,* and the *Vengure,* all belongin' to His Majesty's navy, is layin' off Spithead, round yon bend. They be sailing for Lisbon with the tides, takin' soldiers to Spain." The old man grinned with malice. "Now gets out of here. I got important work to do."

Victoria gazed out at the harbor, as if she might see the navy ships of which the man spoke. All hope was lost, for she couldn't book passage on a naval vessel.

Tired and hungry, she wandered into one of the byways that led away from the docks, looking for lodgings. It was clear she would be in the coastal town much longer than she expected. She might even have to look for employment to supplement her meager funds.

She found a small airless room in the attic of a rather disreputable inn, but the price was right. After a meal of stale bread and cheese and a mug of bitter ale, Victoria decided to walk to the harbor to watch the ships being boarded by those who would be able to leave Portsmouth.

Despite the fading light, the docks were as busy as they had been that morning. She found a spot out of the way and marveled at the beauty of the sun's surrender of the day.

There was still a reddish glow in the western sky when what appeared to be a quarrel broke out some ways away and a jeering crowd soon gathered. Victoria remembered the warning about the press gang and decided the safest thing was to go to her room for the night. She pulled the collar of her wool coat up against the night's bitter wind, then hurried through the alley ways looking for the inn where her small bag was tucked under the bed.

In the darkness, all began to look alike. In a panic, she hurried around the corner of a small alehouse, and straight into a soldier exiting the establishment.

A hand clamped on the back of her collar, nearly lifting her off her feet. "Well, looky what we got here, Jamie."

Victoria found herself in the grasp of a very drunk private. His sour breath made her sick. Desperate to get away, she tugged against his restraining grip. She suddenly wished she'd brought her father's small pistol which was packed in her leather satchel. With little hope, she tried to placate him. "I apologize for bumping into you, sir."

The man's companion, another drunken foot soldier, mocked her. "Well, ain't ye the proper one. Got any blunt to prove yer truly sorry. Me mate 'n me wants to drink a bit longer and we're cleaned out."

The first soldier lifted Victoria completely off the ground. "Yeah, got any coins what me friend and me can use?"

The pillow stuffed into the front of her breeches began to shift about. Victoria wrapped her arms around her midsection, praying she wouldn't lose the cushion, pants, or worse, both of them. "S-sir, I am but a poor servant, looking for employment."

The soldier named Jamie tried to pry her arms free so he might search her coat. "Let me see . . ."

Determined to keep the man's hands from prying too deeply, Victoria began to kick at the drunk, but the soldier only laughed as he continued to prod at her person. She used the only weapon at her disposal, a loud cry for help.

The end of a dueling pistol appeared out of the darkness directly under Jamie's chin. With unbounded relief, Victoria looked up to see a tall gentleman push the searching soldier away. He then turned and spoke in cultured tones to the one who still held her feet off the ground. "I believe you have something that doesn't belong to you, my good man."

Victoria's feet touched the cobblestone, but her knees were shaky as they bore the brunt of her weight. She kept her arms tightly wrapped around her for she was certain the pillow was about to pop out and reveal her masquerade.

Jamie was suddenly all subservient. "Don't be wantin' any trouble, sir. Just havin' a bit a fun with the lad."

Just then an officer stepped into the light spilling from the alehouse door. "I'll have you fellows flogged for thievery."

"Sir, we're just funnin' the lad, we were." Jamie looked at his companion, fear etched on his face.

Victoria, now that she was safe, was appalled at the idea that the men, no matter the circumstances, might be flogged. "Sir, I am unharmed. There is no need."

The major gave a curt nod of his head. "Very well, don't you men have somewhere else you belong?"

Both the inebriated soldiers straightened, then saluted. "That we does, Major." Jamie grabbed his drunker companion and disappeared down the alleyway.

The major looked at Victoria's rescuer. "We have

no time to dawdle, Kit. Hurry or you will miss your ship to Lisbon."

Victoria's heart leapt at the name of the Portuguese town. "Lisbon! Pray, sir, will you take me with you? I should gladly go as your servant."

"I have no need of a servant." The man named Kit put his pistol away.

Victoria, keeping one hand on the ever shifting pillow, placed the other on the arm of the gentleman as he was about to depart, clutching him as if her life depended on it. He was not a soldier, so she wondered how he might be going to Lisbon. However he managed it, she had to convince him to take her along.

"I would work for no wages, sir. Simply let me go with you."

The man turned to look down at her, causing Victoria to stifle a gasp, for he was excessively handsome. From the light of the alehouse she could see dark eyes peering back at her as a generous mouth with even white teeth gave a mirthless grin.

"You would do better finding employment in Portsmouth, boy."

"I *must* go to Lisbon, sir."

"Why would a lad like yourself want to go to Portugal?" One dark brow arched questioningly under a black beaver hat.

Victoria had already devised the story she would use if questioned. The falsehood flowed from her lips with ease. "My father is batman to Captain Rydal, sir. The soldier has written that the old man is quite ill, requesting that I come to bring him home. They are both in Lisbon, sir."

" 'Tis too dangerous for one as young as yourself, by far."

"Sir, I may never again set eyes upon my esteemed

father if you don't allow me to accompany you tonight. No other ship sails for Lisbon in the coming fortnight." Victoria's voice held a note of hysteria, even as she struggled to keep the pitch properly deep. Here was her chance to get to Charles, she couldn't let it slip away. "Please, sir, can you possibly know the loss of a beloved father?"

The dark gaze surveyed her for a long moment. He sighed deeply then said, "Very well. Get your belongings. If you aren't at the Landing dock in thirty minutes, I leave without you. What's your name, boy?"

Victoria hesitated just a moment. "Victor, sir. Victor Woods."

"Well, Victor, you must hurry, for the *Avenge* sails with the tide tonight, and the navy waits for no man."

Victoria hadn't a clue how the civilian gentleman had managed passage on a Royal Navy ship, she only gave thanks to God he would take her with him. Having regained her bearings now, she hurried to find the inn and retrieve her small portmanteau. She must be at the dock on time.

CHAPTER TWO

The rhythmic splash of the oars in the black water beat a steady cadence as the small boat inched towards the *Avenge*. A strong wind blew from the east and countered much of the oarsmen's efforts, but made the small British flag at the rear crackle proudly in the breeze.

Kit was settled comfortably in the middle of the small craft, his trunk and a small portmanteau beside him. He could see his new servant hunched at the bow, clutching a leather satchel as if it held all his worldly goods. Kit questioned the wisdom of allowing the boy to go to Lisbon, but he'd been touched by the effort the young man was making to get to his ailing parent. Reminded of his own father's sudden demise, Kit had relented.

"Put your backs into it, lads," Midshipman Bell called from the stern of the small launch where he stood overseeing the rowing sailors. "We're almost there."

Some ten minutes later the hull of the tiny craft thumped against the oak timbers of the towering *Avenge* as it pitched and rolled in the choppy sea. The oars now pointed skyward as the boat came to the larboard side, allowing the two vessels to come parallel. Kit left his trunk to be brought later, but tossed the portmanteau up to the side boy, whose job it was to help those who boarded. The lad put down the bag, then stood waiting at the rail adjusting the manropes beside the main wale's ladder.

"Victor, your gear."

Young Woods made his way between the oarsmen to the middle of the small boat and handed the bag to Kit, instead of tossing it up on his own. Amused, Kit threw it up to the waiting swabbie, then started to climb on board, calling for Victor to follow him.

Navigating the protruding rungs on the rocking ship, the viscount noted that the gunports on all decks were closed. Often when the navy transported soldiers, the guns on the lower deck were removed to make room for the troops. But as he rose higher he was certain the twenty-four pounders of the middle deck were secured behind the closed gunports, ready for action. Not that it was usual to encounter a French frigate, since the Spanish were now English allies, but one could never be certain.

Moonlight bathed the main deck with a soft silvery sheen aided by small lanterns. The eighteen-pound cannons sat along each wall of the deck. A mixture of red-coated soldiers, some army, others marines, stood about in great huddles talking or giving the shore one last longing perusal. Kit could see the captain on the quarterdeck well above the activities of those boarding. The naval officer stood alone on what Kit had come to think of as holy ground, for no one on board might go on the quarterdeck unless invited by the captain. Major Cooper had informed him the gentleman's name was Dickson.

The side boy, who'd taken their bags, eyed his superior officer, then hearing the captain call him to bring up the viscount, led Kit up the narrow gangway to where the captain stood. The boy then unceremoniously dropped the bags and scurried back to the main deck as the captain dismissed him.

In the dim light from the lanterns it was difficult to make out Captain Dickson's features beneath the black cockaded hat he wore 'fore and aft' when he turned to eye his passengers. "Welcome, to the *Avenge,* Lord Ridgecrest, I believe you were the final person to board. Lt. Hanson, give the order to set sail."

A junior officer on the main deck called to a midshipman, who in turn passed the order. A whistle piped—on the lower deck seamen hurried to the capstan, inserted the bars and began the clockwise motion of raising the anchor. The riggings soon filled with sailors.

The captain paid scant heed, knowing his orders were being carried out. "I have a letter from the Admiralty which informs me you are urgently needed in Lisbon on a matter of importance to the government."

Kit never discussed his reasons for going to the Peninsula with anyone, but he detected no hint of sarcasm from the captain. He'd sailed on several vessels where the commanding officers detested civilians on their ships and had been hostile to Kit, thinking him some young man traveling on a lark and taking advantage of connections at court. He was glad Captain Dickson was not one of those.

"Captain, I know my intruding in this military operation is an inconvenience. My servant and I will take any small space you can allot us even if it must be with the troops on the lower deck." Kit heard Victor shift restlessly behind him. Was the boy afraid to be housed with common soldiers after his encounter near the alehouse?

"That shan't be necessary, my lord. You are in luck, for the admiral does not sail with us on this voyage. His quarters are at your disposal."

This was an unexpected luxury for Kit. Most often he'd been assigned one of the tiny cubicles allotted to the junior officers at the edge of the wardroom. He knew his accommodations would be as spacious as the captain's own, if one could call shipboard cabins such. "That is most kind, Captain."

"Think nothing of it, my lord. But I fear space is at a minimum what with all these soldiers and army gentlemen. Your man will have to use a hammock in your quarters or sleep on deck."

"In my quarters is fine, sir." Kit knew there was room for ten men in the admiral's two rooms.

The captain gave a nod then called, "Mr. Jarrett!"

A boy who looked as sturdy as a tree, with a baby face, scurried onto the quarterdeck and stood perfectly erect, wearing a smaller version of the uniform the naval gentleman wore, with the exception of very little gold braid. "Aye, sir."

"Take Lord Ridgecrest's man to the admiral's quarters and make certain he has a hammock. My lord," the captain again spoke to Kit. "I thought you might wish to remain on deck, then join me for a glass of brandy after we are under way. I should like to introduce my officers to you."

"I would be pleased to join you, sir." Kit turned

to his new servant. "Victor, go with Mr. Jarrett. There is no need to wait up. I can manage for myself this evening." The young man stared at Kit for a moment as if he'd suddenly remembered he was now employed, and not just a fellow traveler.

"Very good, my lord." The boy's voice finally returned in a low tone.

Kit watched his newly acquired servant pick up their bags then follow the cabin boy away. In the darkness, Victor appeared to be about sixteen or so, but to be honest Kit hadn't gotten a good look at the lad. It probably hadn't been the wisest decision to hire him, for now Kit felt responsible for the boy. This mission was too important to jeopardize, but helping the lad get to Lisbon wouldn't impede Kit's journey in the least. Perhaps Victor was too young to be taken to a rough land like Portugal, but he would soon join his father and should the man have died, the young army officer who'd summoned him would be there to take him in hand, then he wouldn't be Kit's worry anymore.

With that thought, he turned to watch as the lights on shore begin to fade. He'd set Jose to keep watch over his mother and sister. Kit was hopeful he would return and find all as he'd left it, or at the very least, no worse than he'd left it. He knew if he was to give his sister the promised Season within the next year or so, he'd have to invest time in the estate which might make this his last trip to the Peninsula.

The ship drew seaward with the receding tide. The unfurling canvas sails filled with wind and the *Avenge* began her voyage to Portugal.

* * *

Victoria had been so excited about finally getting on board a ship bound for Lisbon, she'd given little thought to anything else. But Lord Ridgecrest had just planted her a facer, as Charles would have said. She had hired herself out as a man's servant and he expected her to behave as such. Not only that, but she was to share his cabin. Truth be told, however, the alternative could have been worse. She might have been housed below deck with the common soldiers, with no possibility of privacy.

In a daze, she followed the cabin boy back to the main deck, where he led her through a low doorway. She remembered the viscount's words about taking care of himself that evening, thus putting the problem of Lord Ridgecrest aside for the moment. She stared with interest at the room to which the lad brought her. She had expected something more grand for an admiral, but the ceilings were low with open beams and the chamber held little furniture. Still, she was pleased to see that the small space was spotless. The lacquered wood glistened in the lantern light.

Young Master Jarrett interrupted her inspection of the quarters as he walked to the table in the middle of the room. "This is the outer room for dining and meetings. Back there is the after-cabin where your master sleeps. I shall have one of the sailors bring you a hammock and you can hang it there." He pointed to the corner of the small outer room.

"Thank you."

The cabin boy came around the table. He was a husky lad who stood nearly as tall as Victoria, and she could tell by the look in his brown eyes that he was trouble. "We must come to terms, my good man."

At first Victoria was amused until he began to poke his stubby finger into her pillow-stuffed stomach. "I'll tell you the same thing I told those street urchin drummer boys with the Fifty-First. I am a gentleman's son, and as such, you will address me as *sir*. There are ways of getting a person flogged even on the word of a cabin boy, for as you know *I* am an officer-in-training.''

Victoria's ire rose. She was quite unused to the subservient role she'd chosen, so she pushed the young man's hand away. ''I'll thank you not to do that.''

Drunk with the power he was certain he held over a mere servant, the lad continued in his high-pitched voice. ''I'll not have you kicking up your heels with any larks on board, upsetting the captain and me.''

Victoria'd had enough of the pompous youth. She grabbed his shoulder and thrust him with all her might back to the doorway. Only the element of surprise helped her propel the large boy through the door. ''The only time I might feel it necessary to kick up my heels will be to put my foot into your backside if you don't mind your manners. I would hate to have to speak to the viscount about what a shocking bully you are.'' Releasing the seething boy, she belatedly added, ''Sir.''

With a gentle bang, she shut the door in Mr. Jarrett's flushed face. She dismissed the arrogant brat from her mind as she turned back to the rooms she was to share with Lord Ridgecrest.

The thought of the tall handsome stranger being in such close quarters with her made her spine tingle. She knew she should be shocked beyond all that was proper, but she'd never been one of those missish young females. Her old grandfather often said you took what life delivered you and made the best of it, so that was what she would do. After all, no one ever need know about this little lapse of convention, she tried to convince herself. She would be here and the gentleman would be all the way in the other room.

The floor beneath her tilted then yawed a bit, alerting Victoria that the *Avenge* was now under sail. She hurried through the archway into the second room where she discovered a small door which opened on to a gallery at the rear of the flagship. At the back of the narrow room were windows through which to look out. She turned the latch and opened one, but all there was to see were black waves which seemed to swell as high as the portal where she stood and an ocean of stars above. The English shore could no longer be distinguished against the night sky.

She tried to swallow the great lump which rose in her throat. There was no going back now. Whatever the consequences of her decision to enlist herself as a gentleman's gentleman and sail to Portugal, the die was cast. She would have to do the best she could, without betraying her identity to the handsome young viscount. Once they reached Lisbon, she could disappear into the crowded streets her cousin had written about, and neither Lord Ridgecrest nor Charles ever need know the truth about her journey to Portugal.

A knock sounded on the cabin door. Victoria hoped the obnoxious Mr. Jarrett hadn't returned. She closed the small window, and hurried to answer the summons. A seaman handed her a large folded bundle. "These is fer ye, lad."

Victoria thanked the man and closed the door. She soon discovered it was a hemp cloth bed and blanket with a thin flock pallet which appeared to constitute a mattress. Within a matter of minutes, she hung the brass rings of the hammock on the hooks in the beams near the corner. Realizing it was best to be abed before the viscount returned, she removed her hat, frock coat and shoes before climbing into the swinging bed for the night, pulling the blanket over her.

The gentle rocking of the sailor's roost soon helped Victoria forget her worries. Fatigued from her arduous flight to the south, she soon fell into a dreamless sleep.

Later, a sound awakened her with a start. She lifted her head, and spied the silhouette of a man in the light. Alarmed at first, her memory returned as the sounds of creaking timbers reminded her she was on board the *Avenge*.

The viscount turned a bit to his left and the light gleamed across his handsome face. Her gaze trailed lower and her cheeks warmed. She should look away, but she was intrigued by his masculinity. Unaware he was being observed, the man stood only in his inexpressables, reading some document. She could see he had a powerful well-muscled body with dark hair on his chest.

Against her will, Victoria's gaze traveled the length of the rippled plane of his stomach to where the dark tuft narrowed, then disappeared beneath the band of his pantaloons. Her heart suddenly began to race and her insides felt aflutter. Reluctantly she drew her intrusive gaze away and wondered if it was the gentle sway of the ship which made her feel so strange. She had heard that people could be seasick, but this feeling was not at all unpleasant.

Victoria forced her eyes shut, knowing she shouldn't be peering at a gentleman in such a state of undress. For certain she shouldn't be enjoying such a sight. With a sigh, she wondered what intimate duties she would be expected to perform in the morning. She shivered and tugged the blanket closer before again succumbing to her fatigue.

Kit folded his orders. Questions kept swirling in his head about the mission. All would be clear only after he was at the meeting in Portugal, so he decided to retire.

As he walked over to a chest of drawers to put the orders away, the sway of the hammock in the other room caught his eye. Was the boy finding his sea legs, he wondered? Kit took little notice of the ship's movement, but he knew from experience that those new to sea travel could become dreadfully ill. The gentle swing of the hammock had caused the boy's wool blanket to slip to the floor.

Kit stepped into the outer room, then draped the cover back on the young man, tucking it inside the hammock bed. The lad was an odd one, sleeping fully dressed except for shoes and his outer coat. The viscount contemplated loosening the boy's neck cloth, then he decided Victor was old enough to dress and undress himself. Why did he feel this need to take care of the boy?

He went back into the admiral's bedroom and blew out the candle before settling on the hard bunk. His mind drifted to his mission. If the weather was good, he would be in Lisbon a full week before the meeting with Sir James.

A part of Kit was wary of this rendezvous. Sir James was part of an intricate network of men in the Peninsula who worked for Horse Guards. Why had this informer specifically asked for Kit? Wellington had any number of exploring officers who roved the countryside buying information. It might well be a trap.

Dr. Curtis had confirmed that the French were searching for him. They'd even given him that ridiculous name, the English Phantom.

Kit rolled to his side, staring out the rear windows at the stars that appeared to sway with the motion of the ship. He was certain of only one thing. Wellington was too important to king and country to ignore the possibility of such a plot.

The sun hadn't edged above the horizon when Victoria awoke the following morning. In the grey dawn light, she climbed out of the hammock and switched waistcoats, putting the one on top underneath. She carefully adjusted the pillow to make certain it was secure, then she donned the frock coat and her shoes. She would have to wait until Lord Ridgecrest was dressed, for her call of nature.

She hurried from the room, wanting to be far from his lordship when he did rise. She was not unaware of what was expected of her, having helped with the care of her ill father. She'd even seen a man's bare chest before, but nothing so splendid as what she'd seen in the lantern's glow the previous evening.

She exited the passageway into the crisp morning air. Despite the early hour, seaman were busy with their daily tasks. The decks were being swabbed, sails were being repaired and several seamen climbed through the rigging, adjusting ropes. Small clusters of red-coated soldiers also dotted the decks, up from the lower deck for a bit of fresh air. A lone sailor stood at the ship's wheel, an officer beside him gazing into the distance through a spy glass.

Victoria was drawn to the rail to admire the ocean. There was a vastness to the prospect before her that awed her. In the distance she could see the *Denmark* and the *Vengure,* each on a different tack as they made their way to Portugal.

As the tip of the sun rose above the horizon, Victoria felt a presence at her side. A leathery-skinned sailor, red scarf tied over greying braided pigtails with gold rings at his ears, stood smiling at her with a toothless grin. He wore a faded blue coat and stained canvas pants. " 'Tis a b'ootiful sight, ain't it young fellow." He gestured to the sunrise.

Victoria couldn't resist smiling back at the colourful fellow. "I don't believe I ever saw a lovelier dawn."

"Twenty years I be sailin', and never does I tire of seein' that sun in the morn. In the early days 'twas the fine colors I admired, now I reckon I'm just 'appy to still be 'ere to see 'er rise."

"You've been in many a battle then." She eyed the man with interest. He was a common sailor, and Lady Victoria Woodley could never have stood in conversation with such a man, but Victor Woods could.

"Oh, a fair number, lad. Is this yer first time aboard a ship?"

"That it is. I believe the *Avenge* is a very fine boat."

"Ship, lad, ship. That 'er is. Ye see that on the wall." The old man pointed to the afterpart of the quarter deck.

Victoria could see large bold characters written in gold.

"Can ye read, boy? If not, I'll tell ye the words."

Victoria would have been very much surprised if the rough man beside her could read. She suspected all the sailors on board knew the phrase by heart. " 'England expects every man to do his duty.' "

The sailor nodded his head in satisfaction. "Aye, that's what it says. 'Tis a memento of the late immortal

Lord Nelson's final signal afore we sailed into action
at Trafalgar that day. Only ships what was in the battle
carry them words.''

"Meeks!" A high-pitched voice interrupted the
conversation. "Haven't you work to do?"

Victoria turned to see Mr. Jarrett glaring at her.

The seaman only bobbed his head. "I do, sir." He
then ambled off to the opposite side of the deck.

"Your master seeks you." There was a bit of gloating
in the cabin boy's face as he relayed the message, as
if to remind her of her lower station in life.

Victoria was surprised when the boy merely stared
at her after making the announcement. With the
slender hope that she might appease the little mon-
ster some, she cheerily said, "Good morning, Mr.
Jarrett, sir. Where might I find hot water for the
viscount?"

"You can get water and coffee for Lord Ridgecrest
in the galley. Through that door, down the stairs to
the middle deck and forward near the foremast."
There was no softening in his expression.

She merely thanked the boy then hurried into the
ship's interior, having more to worry about than some
childish schemer. The hallways were narrow and
poorly lit. There was the damp smell of gunpowder
and stale bodies as she made her way forward. She
had no trouble finding the ship's galley. The cook
was an ancient sailor sporting a wooden leg and a
black patch over one eye.

On discovering her to be the viscount's servant,
Cookie, as he called himself, provided her with a
somewhat dented silver pot of coffee, a fine porcelain
cup and saucer, and a can of hot water. He also
offered up a beefsteak and eggs for his lordship and
a bowl of something he called burgoo, which

appeared to be a porridge, for herself. Victoria placed all on a tray the seaman gave her and made her way nervously back to the admiral's room and her new duties.

Kit stood in the gallery behind his cabin looking out at the morning sky. He hoped the weather would remain mild. He'd heard tales of the five-day trip to Lisbon taking as long as three weeks during the storm season. If that happened he would be late for his rendezvous with Sir James. Still, there was no point in worrying about what he couldn't control.

He strolled back into the cabin, deciding to get dressed. He'd been surprised to find Victor gone from his hammock. He'd encountered Mr. Jarrett in the passageway as he poked his head out to look for his servant and requested the cabin boy find young Victor. He hoped his temporary valet was staying out of trouble.

Kit donned a shirt and was tucking the tail into his pantaloons when the door opened and his servant halted on the threshold, a tray balanced in his hands. Kit thought the boy was going to turn and run for a moment. The lad looked frightened of his own shadow, or was he frightened of Kit? Thinking it might be the latter, Kit called in a friendly tone, "Good morning, Victor. Come in. You have just the thing to wake me this morning."

Victor slowly advanced towards the table, eyes on the tray as if he were afraid he might spill its contents. "Good morning, my lord." His voice was low yet soft.

Kit strolled into the main cabin and got his first look at the lad in the light of day. The boy's hair was badly cut and surprisingly a shade darker than the pale brown arched brows. His face was a bit too delicate in features to be called manly, but no doubt that would come with age. Old-fashioned clothes hung loosely on the boy's lumpish body. Whatever the lad had been doing, it hadn't been hard labor. Victor's hands were as fragile and white as his face.

Kit took the cup of coffee offered by the youth, then settled into a seat and began to enjoy his breakfast. Curious, he asked between bites, "Where is your home, Victor?"

The boy's gaze flew to meet his. Kit was startled by the pale green colour. It reminded him of the delicate new growth of leaves in the spring. They were eyes framed with long dark lashes, that, on a woman, might cause a man to forget himself. Damned if he hadn't been too long away from female companionship, Kit thought, and looked away from the boy, concentrating on his steak. The next time he was in London, he should find a bit of muslin to amuse himself, he decided.

"The north, my lord."

Kit chuckled. "That covers a great deal of territory from where we stand."

"Near Carlisle, sir."

"Ah, I have never been in that part of the country."

Kit could have little notion how relieved his servant was to hear that. Victoria was curious about the man she traveled with. There was that about him, his dark hair and eyes, that looked Spanish, yet he carried an English title. She, as a servant, could ask no prying personal questions. Instead she inquired as to the length of the journey, and was informed that with good weather they could reach Lisbon in four and a half days.

She removed the tray with her food from the table,

knowing she was far too nervous of her duties to eat at the moment. When the viscount had finished his breakfast, she was quite prepared. "Are you ready to finish dressing, my lord?"

The viscount looked at her with a grin. "Dare I trust a greenling like yourself with my razor."

Victoria knew her skill to be sure. After her father's valet had returned from a short illness, her parent still preferred his daughter's more gentle touch. "My lord, I have never nicked a gentleman I served."

Lord Ridgecrest turned his chair around then again settled, crossing his long outstretched legs at the ankles. "Then, my boy, I am at your mercy." He closed his eyes and tilted back his head.

Victoria hurried to where the viscount's trunk sat unpacked. She chided herself for having forgotten to do it the night before. She was proving to be an inefficient valet. She retrieved a small leather case which held a straight razor, sandalwood-scented soap, and small brush. Finding a towel packed as well, she utilized the cloth to cover the gentleman's fine linen shirt. Then with a dab of the hot water, she used the brush to work up a good lather with the soap.

She stepped forward. Her hand hovered just a moment over the handsome face. She reminded herself, it was no different than shaving her father. In fact, it should be easier. The planes of the viscount's face were smoother. She quickly covered his strong jaw with lather, then picked up the razor.

Still, she hesitated.

"Well, get on with it, lad, before the soap dries."

"Y-yes, my lord." Victoria took a deep breath. The cold blade glided smoothly over his cheek, despite the fact that Victoria now felt breathless as her fingers pressed against his warm chin to steady his jaw. She bit down on her lip, and carefully continued her task. As the lather was scraped away, she admired his rugged good looks. There was inherent strength in his face, even thought his firm jaw had just a touch of the stubborn about it. This was the face of a man you could rely on no matter what. She'd known very few such men. Her father had been a weak man, who'd given in to all his human frailties—excessive drink, gaming and heaven knew what. Even Charles, despite his good qualities, had left her to pursue his career in the army.

As she drew the razor over the last bit of soapy foam, she took in every line and hollow, every angle and curve. She didn't know why, but somehow she knew his face would remain in her memory long after he'd disappeared from her life.

The viscount opened one eye. Catching her gazing intently at him, he teased, "Am I bleeding profusely?"

Victoria gathered her wits as she took a ragged breath then stepped away. "Not a nick, as I promised. I was merely thinking you look more a Spanish conquistador than an English viscount, my lord."

His lordship's brows drew slightly together. "Conquistador? Ah, I see you detect my Portuguese ancestry."

She took the cloth from round his neck, then dipped the end in the warm water, and wiped the excess soap from the gentleman's face, trying not to enjoy the task too much. "Finished, sir."

Lord Ridgecrest rose and looked in the mirror. "Excellent, Victor. Now, I shall go up on deck. Make certain my evening clothes are taken out to remove the wrinkles, for I dine with the captain this evening."

"Yes sir."

The viscount quickly tied his cravat in a simple

knot, then donned a tan waistcoat and topped it with a dark brown coat. As his servant watched, the gentleman picked up his hat and exited the room.

Victoria collapsed into a chair. Things were starting to get complicated. Why had a simple shave made her knees feel so weak? She'd performed the task numerous times for her ailing father. Now her wits were positively to let as she sat staring out the rear window wondering at her own discomposure.

CHAPTER THREE

Some twenty minutes passed before Victoria had her thoughts ordered enough to begin her day's tasks. Lord Ridgecrest had informed her he was to dine with the captain. Would he want to wash before he dressed? Was she to see a great deal more of the muscular body beneath the gentleman's clothes? A vision of him glistening with water in the lantern light filled her mind. The image made her quite breathless.

She shoved the unwanted vision aside, knowing that no proper young lady would allow such wanton thoughts. She had the entire day to get through before she needed to help his lordship dress for dinner. She rose and made up the bed where Lord Ridgecrest had slept. Running her hand over the coverlet, the image of the gentleman reclining on the hard bunk caused her to stamp her foot in frustration.

"Victoria Woodley, have you left your reason in England?" Pushing the image of the gentleman from her thoughts once more, she began to unpack the viscount's clothes. She took out his evening clothes and laid them on the bunk, forcing her mind to concentrate on getting out the wrinkles.

The remaining clothes and personal items in the portmanteau and trunk she put in the wardrobe against the wall. Victoria assumed that Lord Ridge-crest must be going to Lisbon to visit family members, for she could think of no other reason to go to a country in the throes of war.

She worked busily at putting away the shaving supplies and cleaning the small cabin, aware of the constant rock of the floor beneath her, but unaffected by the motion. The viscount must have no reason to regret his act of kindness in bringing her along.

With her tasks complete and the dishes returned to the galley, Victoria went up on deck and sat down on one of the large wooden crates of military supplies lashed to the deck between the cannons. It was a good vantage point from which to admire the ocean, yet remain out of the way of the sailors who each seemed to have jobs on which they were intent.

She was soon lost in thought about how angry Charles would be with her at first. But she was certain she could make him understand the serious nature of Uncle Orson's determination to steal her legacy. Charles had achieved his dream, a career in the army. She only wanted an estate which she could run properly and not live married to a fool while her funds were squandered on ridiculous schemes or worse, gamed away.

The sounds of children's voices interrupted Victoria's musings. Three boys, appearing to range between the ages of six and ten, came from below decks. Dressed in uniforms of yellow with gold trim she recognized them as the drummer boys for the

Fifty-First. The crew paid little heed to the lads, but Victoria's heart ached at the thought of boys at such a tender age witnessing the carnage on a battlefield even though they wouldn't fight.

At present they were carefree and laughing, and they found a spot in the excess cargo on deck to begin a game of toss-penny using the wall of the gunwale. They were wagering no sums, having just the three coins they played with, the bragging rights to the winner being the only reward.

Victoria watched them for several minutes, amused at the fun they derived from the simple game. As she turned back to admire the sea, she noted the captain, Lord Ridgecrest and the commanding officer of the Fifty-First had come up on the quarterdeck. Their conversation was carried away on the wind, but by the grim look on their faces she was certain that the three gentlemen spoke of the war. She would love to hear how England was faring in the conflict which had been going since '08, but as a valet she'd set herself apart from the Quality.

Despite her best intention to put the gentleman from her mind, Lord Ridgecrest drew her gaze. Tall and well built, he was impressive even in the company of the ornately uniformed men. She thought it best she keep her distance over the course of the voyage, for clearly she was not blind to his attraction as a man.

A familiar high-pitched voice disturbed her musings. Behind her, Mr. Jarrett had come upon the drummer boys' game and was intent on mischief. "There's no gaming onboard the *Avenge.* I'm taking that money and *ordering* the lot of you below."

The oldest boy, a tow-headed lad of ten, stepped

between the cabin boy and the coins on the deck. "Ye ain't takin' our blunt ye ocean goin' water rat."

The two youngest boys huddled beside the cargo box, afraid to confront the young naval tyrant who towered above them, but one found the courage to try and save his coin. "Don't let 'im take 'um, Benny. They're ours."

Mr. Jarrett reached out a beefy hand and shoved young Benny to the deck and scooped up the coins. "No gaming. Captain's rules." He then dropped the coins in his pocket, a smirk on his spotty face.

Victoria's temper flared. She was certain that the conniving 'officer-in-training' had every intention of stealing the smaller boys' money. She jumped down to intercede but young Benny was before her. He had more courage than size, and bounded up from the deck and barrelled into the cabin boy.

The two hit the planking and began rolling about, throwing wild punches which generally missed their target, but occasionally a fist met with an eye or a nose and blood appeared on both faces. The surrounding sailors and soldiers on deck formed a ring about the fighting boys, calling for the lad of their choice to prevail.

Victoria pushed her way through the throng of shouting men. She was appalled that not a single man made an effort to stop the fight. Fearful that the smaller Benny would take the lion's share of blows, she stepped into the ring of men and attempted to stop the fray.

Unfortunately, the boys' flailing legs tangled with Victoria's as she came near and she tumbled down into the middle of the amateur bout of fisticuffs with a thud. In a flash, Mr. Jarrett had planted her two quick blows to the breadbasket, as Charles would have said, and Victoria, despite the cushioning of the pillow found herself without wind and rolled to her back on the deck. Benny and young Jarrett, still thrashing about, rolled on top of her, and she was sure she would never catch her breath again.

A loud voice roared nearby. "Cease your fighting at once."

Both boys halted in an instant, rolling to either side of Victoria. All three sat staring at Captain Dickson, Lord Ridgecrest and the colonel of the regiment, uncertain who had issued the command. The army officer, with arms akimbo, barked, "Stand up, the lot of you."

The two boys jumped to their feet and stood erect. Victoria, still struggling to catch her breath was slower. As she straightened her coat, she saw that the boys' blood was now smeared on her outer vest and shirt. Looking up, she could see a look somewhere between amusement and displeasure in the viscount's dark gaze.

The colonel glared at the trio. "What is the meaning of this barbaric display?"

Mr. Jarrett addressed himself to his superior officer. "They was gaming, Captain. I tried to stop 'em."

The colonel's grey brows drew together as he turned to Benny and Victoria. "Were you not told that there was to be no gaming on board?"

Victoria thought Benny was about to cry, but he merely nodded his head and parroted, "Yes, sir."

"Did I not say that any man caught gaming would be flogged?"

Horrified at what the spiteful Mr. Jarrett was about to accomplish, Victoria rushed to the boy's defend. "Sir, the lads weren't gaming."

Certain she looked a complete ruffian, Victoria felt

herself under the measuring gaze of the colonel. "Who are you? Were you involved in this matter?"

Mr. Jarrett leaned forward. "He wasn't even here. He don't know what he's talking about. I tell you they were gaming."

The red-coated officer eyed the trio and grunted a "harrumph," then turned to the captain. "There's no knowing which is telling the truth. Flog the lot of 'em is my method. Teach 'em to stay out of trouble."

Victoria's heart plummeted. Was she about to be unmasked here? In the guise of a servant her word held less credence to the officers than the detestable young cabin boy, him being from a genteel family.

Lord Ridgecrest stepped forward, contempt on his face as he eyed the officer. "Colonel, is the army in the habit of using the lash for what appears to be a childish misunderstanding. I would hear the truth from Victor. He has no reason to lie."

With knees trembling, Victoria struggled to keep her voice properly pitched. She breathed a prayer of thanks for the viscount's kind heart, for he knew practically nothing about her, yet in fairness gave her a chance. "My lord, it is as you have said. The lads from the Fifty-First were playing a simple game. I was watching from yon crate. They were using coins as tossing tokens, not for wagering. I fear Mr. Jarrett saw the money and mistook it for a wagering game. When he tried to confiscate the money, a fight ensued and I tried to stop the bout, but I was inadvertently drawn in. Truly there was no harm meant by either boy."

Victoria knew she'd altered the truth somewhat, because she wasn't truly certain Mr. Jarrett's motives were so pure. But unlike him, she could not do another a harm and clearly the colonel was fond of laying on the cat-o'-nine-tails for punishment.

Captain Dickson nodded, then finally spoke. "Thank you, Victor, for helping untangle the matter. I see no reason to enlist the lash over such a trifling misunderstanding. I suggest, Colonel Waring, that your lads return below and Mr. Jarrett return to his duties—as you all should do." He said the last to the men gathered and they immediately began to disperse.

As Mr. Jarrett turned to go, Victoria grabbed the sleeve of his coat. In an undertone, "Give back those coins, or I shall go to the captain and tell him you weren't so innocent."

With a scowl of dislike, the boy dug in his pocket and shoved the coins into Benny's bloody hand before walking away. The army lad grinned at his savior as much as his swollen lip would allow. "Thank ye, sir."

Victoria stood nervously eyeing Lord Ridgecrest, who'd moved closer. She put up her hand to cover her face as he scrutinized her closely, fearful he might see more than she wished about her.

"Well, Victor, I don't think there is any serious damage to your person."

Relieved that his tone was pleasant, Victoria still felt guilty. "My lord, I do apologize for involving myself in matters that didn't concern me and thereby involving you."

Kit clapped a hand on Victor's shoulder. He'd been impressed with the lad's spirited action. "My boy, never apologize for doing the honourable thing. A man is nothing if he has no honour. 'Tis clear you have much to learn about the brutality of military justice, however. Have a care in Lisbon. The place is teeming with soldiers. Take my advice and have at least one gentleman on your side before you wade into a fray.''

Victor bowed and backed toward the companionway to the admiral's cabin. "I shall remember, my lord, but I'd best get myself cleaned up."

Kit watched the boy hurry back to the cabin. For all his fragile appearance, the lad had pluck and that would take him a long way. The danger was that the boy's youthful idealism might be his downfall in a rough town like Lisbon.

Victoria got little sleep that night due to the horror of what might have been the outcome of the boys' fight. Not just the matter of the boys being brutally punished, but her masquerade coming to light. The last thing she needed to do was draw attention to herself in such a manner.

She owed his lordship a double thanks for the outcome of the incident. One for being the kind of man who wouldn't quietly stand by and countenance the flogging of mere children. A second thanks for his kindness to her after she'd drawn him into the matter with her own foolish involvement.

Rising early, Victoria realized at once that the motion of the ship was stronger. She made no mention of the matter to Lord Ridgecrest, who was up as well and seemed unfazed by the steeper pitch of the rising and falling floor. She quickly brought his breakfast from the galley and made herself busy as he ate.

Her hands were steadier as she shaved him, yet there was something in his nearness that caused a strange flutter in her stomach. He was soon dressed and out of the cabin, a thing Victoria was certain could only serve her peace of mind.

She gathered the dirty dishes, stacking them neatly on the tray to return to Cookie. Suddenly, the knife with which Lord Ridgecrest had eaten seemed to fly off the plate.

Victoria hurried to retrieve the utensil, realizing that the ship was rocking a great deal more than when she'd risen. She put the knife on the plate then lifted the fully loaded tray. She struggled to keep the crockery from falling to the floor as she reeled back and forth with the pitch of the ship.

When she stepped into the open air of the main deck, Victoria could see that the sky was now dark grey and the ocean looked ominously black. The ship appeared to settle into a valley of water. Her heart rose in her throat. The vessel which had seemed so large upon boarding seemed dwarfed by the surrounding waters. There was no rain, but the deck was wet from the spray of the large waves. The ship pitched back to the left, making Victoria stagger, even as she hung onto the tray of dishes.

A hand closed over her arm. "Steady there, Victor. Being a sure-footed seaman takes a bit of getting used to. I'm afraid we're in for a bad storm." Lord Ridgecrest smiled reassuringly at her, then signaled to a nearby sailor. "Take this tray to the galley."

The seaman hurried forward and deftly took the tray. He gave a broad wink to the gentleman. "Might want to lash the lad to the riggin', sir, him bein' a bit new to the tricks of the sea."

As the sailor hurried away, the viscount pointed to a spot sheltered from the wind and spray. "If you intend to stay on deck awhile, it might be best to find a secure place to hold on to."

Victoria hurried to the gunwale and grasped the rigging, peering out at the churning water. It was frightening to watch the rise and fall of the walls of water beside the ship, yet exhilarating to feel the sea spray on her face. There was no sign of the *Denmark* or the *Vengure*.

She detected the faint scent of sandalwood and glanced up to see Lord Ridgecrest had joined her. His face held an intent look as he scanned the waves, sending a tremor of some undefinable emotion down her spine. "My lord, are we in danger?"

His dark eyes scanned her face, then his mouth quirked into a half-smile. "My boy, you may find this hard to believe, but I have actually seen the seas far worse and with a less able seafarer than Captain Dickson. I think there is little to fear from the storm except our being delayed and experiencing some unpleasant conditions over the next few days." As the gentleman looked back at the churning water, a frown settled on his face.

Overwhelmed with the sudden desire to smooth the wrinkles from his handsome brow, Victoria knew that to do so might get her into waters far more dangerous than the ones before her. She must not allow herself to be drawn to a man she would never see again after they docked in Lisbon. Forcing her gaze back to the ocean, she made light of the matter. "Well sir, for myself, I can say, 'If we do not find anything very pleasant, at least we shall find something new.'"

Suddenly she felt the gentleman's gaze on her, as intently as he'd formerly stared at the dark seas. She decided it best that she leave. Discounting the strange effect he had on her, there was a searching quality in his bold stare that made her wary. "Is there anything I can do for you, my lord, before I return to the cabin?"

He was quiet for so long, Victoria thought he hadn't

heard the question above the sound of the wind and the flap of the sails. At last, he offered gruffly, "No, the day is yours to do with as you will."

Kit watched as the boy weaved his way back to the companionway which led to the cabin they shared. The quote Victor had recited struck a familiar note. Kit felt a gnawing sensation deep in the pit of his stomach. He wasn't sure what it was, but there was something about the young man that bothered him.

He turned back to the rail and gazed out at turbulent waters, trying to determine what it was about Victor that had set him on edge. He was suddenly jostled by a passing seaman.

"Sorry, my lord." Lt. Hanson tugged at his hat while he stared up at the sails.

"Mr. Hanson, do you read a great deal?" Kit thought the young officer just might be able to help.

"There is little else to do, my lord, when one is at sea." The lieutenant eyed Kit with a pleasant arch of one pale sun-bleached brow.

"Can you refresh my memory? Are you familiar with the quote 'If we do not find anything very pleasant, at least we shall find something new'?"

"Indeed, sir. 'Tis a favorite of mine. The line comes from Voltaire's *Candide*. I have a copy if you should like to borrow it."

"Thank you," Kit replied distractedly. The young officer offered to bring the book to his lordship's cabin after his watch, then walked off to continue his duties, but Kit scarcely gave more than a nod of his head. His mind was on the lad he'd helped get onboard the *Avenge*. A young servant from the wilds of northern England who quoted a French philosopher.

Then Kit remembered something else that had bothered him the day before. Victor had commented that Kit looked like a conquistador. How many servants knew what the devil a conquistador was, much less could say the word without stumbling? Victor spoke in as cultured a tone as any gentleman Kit had ever encountered.

As a particularly large gust of wind carried a heavy mist over the rail, Kit moved away from the edge, finding shelter near the doorway. He was distracted a moment watching Mr. Hanson give several seamen orders, calling each by name. The burly seamen seemed to respect the young officer.

Kit had sailed on enough of His Majesty's vessels to know that Mr. Hanson's firm but humane treatment of his men wasn't always the rule. A brutal officer like Colonel Waring could make life miserable for the men under him. Floggings were still a common occurrence in the British Army and Navy. It was a practice Kit abhorred and he was puzzled that a gentleman's son could behave with so little compassion for his inferiors.

A gentleman's son.

The words echoed in his brain. That was what bothered him about Victor. The boy behaved more like a member of the Quality than some underling. He had a way of looking directly at one with those pale green eyes, like an equal, not downcast or reserved like a servant. Kit was beginning to wonder if he'd been tricked. Was it possible that Victor was some gentleman's son, determined to join the army by any means possible?

Or was it, Kit sighed, that all his own involvement in the subterfuge and deceit of this cursed war was causing him to imagine duplicity everywhere he looked? As the ship tacked back to the left, Kit shifted his weight to keep his balance. He only knew he must

watch the boy closely. It galled Kit to think he might
have been so easily gulled. If the lad was some young
sprig of nobility out to defy his father by becoming
a common soldier, Kit would have him on a ship
heading back to England before the *Avenge* had
unloaded a single redcoat.

Rough seas and high winds continued to plague
the *Avenge* during the following week. Kit began to
think he wouldn't make the scheduled rendezvous
with Sir James and the informant. His worry about
the meeting distracted him from his suspicions of
Victor, but when at last the weather relented and the
ship was under full sail and nearing the Portuguese
coast, Kit knew he must come to some decision about
what must be done in regard to his young servant.

Kit tried to covertly observe Victor over the course
of the journey and was now convinced that the young
man was of high birth. The boy's refined, almost
feminine features and his cultured speaking practically screamed, if not nobility, at least gentility. The
few times he'd caught Victor unawares on deck, Kit
had tried to draw him out, but discovered a young
man with a quick mind. A mind too quick to be drawn
into betraying the least bit of information about himself. Kit's inquiring questions had elicited a great deal
about Carlisle and the surrounding area, but nothing
of a personal nature about Victor, other than the tale
of an ailing father and the gentleman he served.

On the eleventh day at sea, Captain Dickson
informed Kit that they would reach the Tagus River
the following morning. If their luck held, they would
be unloading the soldiers at Fort Julian by noon. It
was then that the plan came to Kit.

"Captain, I need a message taken to a Captain Rydal as soon as we drop anchor."

Dickson looked at the young gentleman beside him. The naval officer was no fool. He'd asked no questions about the viscount's reason for coming to Portugal, but the very fact that he was traveling via government orders left little doubt that Ridgecrest was set upon secret business.

"Is it a matter of some urgency?"

"Extremely urgent, sir." Kit had government affairs to handle, but having been responsible for getting the boy on board the *Avenge*, he wouldn't feel right until he'd turned Victor over to Captain Rydal. "I should like word sent to headquarters at Belem for the gentleman to meet me at *El Azul Flores* in Black Horse Square as soon as my servant and I land."

Kit chose an inn where he often stayed when passing through Lisbon. The innkeeper assumed he bought and sold wine for his late father's exporting company and asked no questions.

"I'll have a small launch sent ashore as soon as we enter the Tagus River."

"Thank you, Captain." Kit knew he would need to keep a close watch on Victor the following morning. It would be a simple matter to lose one's self in the narrow winding streets of Lisbon. Kit's suspicions might be unfounded, but he wasn't going to take any chances.

At the age of five and twenty Captain Charles Rydal was a young man who knew what he wanted. He wanted a career in the army. He wanted to distinguish himself on the field of battle and he wanted the Dona Incs de la Coelho.

He'd met the young widow at a small gathering
that Colonel Applewood and his wife had thrown for
some of the wounded officers during the Yule Season.
Mrs. Applewood lived in Lisbon while her husband
was in the field and had cultivated many of the locals.
The Dona Ines was one of the Portuguese ladies who
moved in both the more restrictive social world of
local society and among the British community of
the town. She spoke excellent, if somewhat accented,
English.

The depth of his attraction for the unknown beauty
had bowled him over. Never much in the petticoat
line, he'd often thought it foolish to fancy one's self
in love with every pretty face, for there were so many.
But Dona Ines was so much more. Over the course
of the many weeks he'd courted her, he'd discovered
she was well read, not afraid to voice her opinion
without being abrasive, yet would listen to a fair argument of one who would change her views.

He drew the borrowed carriage and horses to a halt
in front of the villa which sat high on the Lisbon
hillside. A small urchin who looked like many of the
Portuguese children, dirty and ragged, ran to take
the head of the soldier's horses knowing there would
be a coin for him when the gentleman left.

Charles stepped down slowly so as not to jar his
injured leg. He straightened his scarlet jacket, put
his hat under his arm and smoothed his blond hair
before rapping sharply on the thick wooden door.
He was not a man of great height, standing barely
five and a half feet, but what he lacked in inches
were make up for by a square muscular build. To
his surprise the oak portal opened immediately and
Dona Ines stood behind a servant, looking ravishing

in a blue silk gown trimmed with lace the same shade of black as that which draped over her mantilla.

"Bom tarde, Capitão Rydal."

Charles liked the sound of his name on the lady's lips. He stepped into the dark interior and kissed the widow's hand with a gallantry he'd never before applied to any woman. "Good afternoon. You are looking lovely as usual, madam."

"Thank you, *Capitão*. Shall we go?" She signaled an old woman who stood in the shadows holding a black velvet cape with blue lining which Senhora de la Coelho quickly donned.

Charles led the lady to his carriage, then settled her comfortably before he paused, frowning as he placed one booted foot on the step. "I fear I cannot take you to Sintra this fine afternoon as we planned. I've received a message from an English viscount who just arrived, requesting I call on him at the Blue Flowers Inn. Can't think why, for I've never met the fellow in my life, but my colonel says he's the Duke of Townsend's heir and I must see what he wants. Do you object, dear lady?"

Dona Ines smiled at the soldier with no guile. "I enjoy riding with you for the company, *Capitão*, not the scenery."

Charles tossed the dirty urchin a coin before he climbed up beside the beautiful lady, savoring her delicate scent of jasmine and life in general. He set the carriage toward the center of town in the direction of the inn where he was to meet with Viscount Ridgecrest, with scarcely a thought as to what the unknown nobleman wanted with him.

* * *

Victoria struggled with the bags as she hurried to keep up with Lord Ridgecrest. The gentleman had made little use of her services as a valet on the voyage. Yet here she was lugging his heavy portmanteau through the muddy Portuguese street on the way to the inn where he would stay. Thankfully his lordship's trunk would come later.

She'd been relieved when he'd casually requested that she accompany him to an inn where he promised to give her directions to Belem—the military headquarters. The city looked immense from the harbor.

As the ship had come to anchorage, a sailor had informed Victoria that Lisbon was a city built on the same number of hills as Rome, but one couldn't see that sitting in the harbor. The Portuguese capital had appeared as one vast high hill with buildings rising one above the other until the summit.

A fine covering of moisture formed on Victoria brow as they trudged the inclining street. The heavy layers of clothing which had been welcomed in the cold English winter were somewhat stifling in the milder Portuguese clime. She would be quite happy to discard her disguise once she was with her cousin.

As she followed his lordship up the hillside away from the harbor, the stench of the streets became almost unbearable. The buildings which had seemed so pristine and white from the water now looked squalid and unkempt. The people appeared unwashed, uneducated and uninterested in strangers as they hurried about their business. In the small street markets, the locals chattered in a language which was completely unintelligible to Victoria, who only spoke French and a bit of Latin.

For the first time since leaving Stoneleigh Manor, Victoria was truly wary. The idea of traveling through these streets without the security of a companion as she searched for Charles almost made her wish to be back in England, but knowing what her uncle had planned, she straightened her back and trudged onward. Her father's small pistol nestled underneath the clothes in her portmanteau gave her a measure of comfort. She would deal with whatever she had to.

At last, they came to a large square with a fountain in the center. Black and white paving stones were cleverly set into the ground to look like waves on the oceans. But Lord Ridgecrest paid scant attention to the uniqueness of the square, as he led her to an inn across the plaza. His lordship was greeted like an old friend, in Portuguese, by a man who hurried forward to welcome them. The viscount answered in the same language, though he exhibited more reserve than the man he called Senhor Braga.

After several minutes of what Victoria could only imagine was polite conversation, the innkeeper, a short, dark-skinned man, led them to a large private parlor at the rear of the inn. The room was lit only by the daylight flooding through two large double doors that opened onto a terrace overlooking the Tagus River.

It wasn't until the innkeeper closed the door that she discovered the private room wasn't empty. A man in uniform rose from a chair. Her heart plummeted.

What surprised Victoria most was not that it was Charles, looking paler and slightly thinner than when she'd last seem him, but that his disinterested gaze had swept over her and failed to recognize his own cousin. She knew, like many people of their class, servants were of no more interest than the furniture.

Her knees began to shake for she knew he was going to be very angry when he discovered her identity.

"Lord Ridgecrest," Charles clicked his heels and bowed. "Captain Rydal, at your service, sir. Allow me to present my companion, Senhora Ines de la Coelho."

A dark-haired woman of incredible beauty rose from a chair beside Charles. Lord Ridgecrest spoke to her in her own language and she nodded her head graciously, before extending her hand to his lordship. When that gentleman bent to place a kiss upon the black glove, admiration was evident in his dark eyes. Victoria suddenly wished that she was not disguised as a man as she took in the lady's elegant attire.

" 'Tis a pleasure to meet you, senhora, Captain. Thank you for coming so promptly."

There was a moment of silence as if each man were waiting for the other to speak. At last, Charles cleared his throat, a slight impatience in his tone. "There is some service I can render you, my lord?"

Kit was puzzled. The captain acted like he'd never seen Victor before and the boy was standing like a statue, a blank look in his green eyes. It was clear neither intended to address the other so Kit did. "Sir, I apologize for intruding on your time. I was led to believe that you were anxiously awaiting the arrival of my traveling companion."

The officer's gaze trailed over to Victor, a look of inquiry on his square-jawed face. The look suddenly veered to one of surprise, then anger. He advanced menacingly on the boy. "What the devil are you doing in Portugal, Vic? Have you taken leave of your senses? Why, I've a mind to turn you over my knee and give you the spanking Uncle Gilbert always threatened, but neglected to give you. Have you come here still in the sulks over not inheriting Stoneleigh?"

Kit was amazed when Victor dropped the bags he'd been clutching and drew his small hands into fists, moving to a stance that even Gentleman Jackson would have praised. "I shall draw your cork, Charles Rydal, just like I did in Carlisle if you dare lay a hand on me."

"It was a demme lucky punch because you know I wasn't even looking at you at the time."

"It's not my fault that just when you told me to swing, you suddenly had to gawk at some fellow in a cavalry uniform who came to call on Papa."

Kit realized at once that the bickering between the pair had the ring of family who'd grown up in close proximity. His hunch about Victor had been correct. The boy was no servant. He and Charles Rydal appeared to be related.

"I simply stopped to speak to Major Wright who'd come to pluck your father one last time, like every other Captain Sharp that visited the estate. You Woodleys always did have more hair than sense when it came to—" Charles stopped suddenly, seeming to really look at his cousin. "What the devil have you done to yourself? You look like you've been working as a climbing boy in London."

"Little you'd care if I had been."

"Confound it, Vic, you've done it now, coming over here. What maggot got into your brain . . ." The captain stopped and looked at his cousin then back at Ridgecrest, a sudden belligerence on his angular face. "Come to think of it, how did my cousin come to be here in your company, my lord?"

Kit knew he was about to be drawn into the argument. "I must take the blame, Captain. Victor duped

me into believing his father was your manservant and
you had requested he come to take care of the old
man. I hired him to act as my valet. Actually for a
young man of birth, he made a conscientious servant.''

"Victor! You think this is Victor?''

Kit was suddenly wary. The captain's tone was skep-
tical. The officer grabbed his young cousin roughly
by the arm and dragged him to stand in front of Kit.
He yanked the boy's hat from his head.

Kit gazed into those pale green eyes and was filled
with a strong foreboding.

''My lord, it would appear you have been doubly
duped. Allow me to introduce your traveling companion. This is my cousin, Lady Victoria Woodley, daughter of the late Earl of Stonebridge.''

CHAPTER FOUR

Kit felt as if someone had knocked his legs out from beneath him. He stared speechless at this person who'd traveled with him for nearly a fortnight, but a complete stranger glared back with defiance.

Victor was a woman! Not Victor, but Victoria!

The words echoed in his brain. Kit felt an utter fool. As a British agent he'd trained himself to see what other's didn't and he'd allowed a female to completely dupe him. A tight knot formed in his chest, a mixture of outrage and disbelief as he stared her up and down with incredulity.

In his own defense, he realized that there was little about her person to betray her—no feminine curves exposed by the man's attire, no missish behavior. Good Lord, the chit had even taken part in a brawl on the ship. There was nothing about her to make one suspect a masquerade.

Well, that wasn't exactly true. Those pale green eyes with long dark lashes had caught his attention, but he'd dismissed them, his mind so full of other matters. He watched as the rebellious look left the lady's face and she began to worry her full lower lip between her teeth.

Then a stark realization dawned. He'd been traveling with an unmarried, unchaperoned female. Not just any female, mind you, but the daughter of an earl. Honour demanded he wed this chit who'd slept in his cabin during the voyage, helped him disrobe and shaved him. His mind reeled at this new complication. Fate had dealt him a leveling blow that fateful night in Portsmouth by putting this hoyden in his path.

With a great effort, he dug deep into his self-control to remember his manners and gave her a stiff bow. "My lady."

Silence again reigned, then the captain stepped into the breech. "Well, Vic, what do you have to say for yourself? I think considering the disastrous predicament you have wrought, his lordship deserves an answer."

Victoria took a deep breath. This wasn't supposed to be happening. She'd thought the viscount would never know about her deceit. She felt an absolute beast for having gotten him into this mess. "Lord Ridgecrest, I owe you a sincere apology but I was desperate when we met. I know you can have little interest in the affairs of the Woodley family which precipitated my leaving my home—"

Charles snorted, interrupting his cousin. "You poor deluded child, don't you understand what you have done? His lordship is about to be intimately concerned with your affairs because of your little escapade. You're lucky he's a proper gentleman. Were it me you'd played this trick on, I'd be more likely to throttle you than marry—"

The viscount put out a hand to stop the soldier's speech. In a cool tone, Ridgecrest said, "I believe what your cousin is trying to tell you, Lady Victoria, is that you are about to become my wife."

Victoria was appalled. It was clear by the viscount's bitter tone that such a marriage was the last thing he wanted. She backed away from the men. "T-there is no need for such a drastic step, my lord. You and I both know that nothing passed between us which would require us to wed."

Ridgecrest's features hardened. "You have often been in the company of other gentlemen as they disrobed?"

Victoria felt her cheeks warm. "N-no, my lord, never but . . . I mean." She raised her chin defiantly. "You hadn't the slightest inkling that I was not Victor Woods, your valet. So how could something of a immoral nature have passed between us?"

His face a mask of stone, the viscount shook his head at her naivety. "Lady Victoria, it is never about what truly happens when a man and woman are together as we were, only about the possibility of what could occur that titillates Society and ruins a female's reputation."

Victoria was desperate. She could tell by the way Charles was nodding his head in agreement that he and Lord Ridgecrest were going to force her into this marriage. As she stared up into the viscount's stern face, she knew it wasn't a union with him that frightened her so. In truth over the past weeks she'd found him to be the most fascinating and handsome man of her acquaintance. For that very reason she didn't want to force him into a loveless marriage knowing her own heart wouldn't remain unaffected.

What a misery it would be to have a husband who despised one. She had run away from just such a forced union herself. He would always blame her for taking his freedom. She struggled not to cry as her throat tightened with the threat of tears.

"B-but the only people who know we were together are you and Charles and of course the senhora there. Surely none of you will say anything. I tell you there is no need for a wedding."

"Do the servants at your estate not know that you have run away?" Ridgecrest's tone was impatient as if he were speaking with a errant child. "Other relatives? I suspect that rumors are already rife in Carlisle about your disappearance, *if* that is where you are truly from."

Victoria suddenly felt as if she were being treated like some simpleton who had to be protected from her mindless actions. "I care not what my relatives have to say of my disappearance, sir, for they deserve no such consideration. As for the people of Carlisle, I seriously doubt any one of them has a clue as to who I am, nor do they care if I ran off with a monkey's uncle. I won't marry you or anyone one else. I think I have made myself clear on this subject and do not wish to hear another word on the matter." Saying that, she turned and marched out of parlour onto the terrace with all the grandeur of a queen exiting from her subjects.

When Captain Rydal, an angry scowl on his face, started towards the door his cousin had exited through, Kit stopped him. "Allow me to handle this, sir." He walked to the portal then stopped. "I must leave for Campo Mayor by nightfall. I have urgent business that cannot be delayed even for the sake of your cousin's good name, therefore, I would suggest that you find us a clergyman, at once.''

Charles stood speechless as the viscount followed Victoria onto the terrace. Campo Mayor was on the frontier and scarcely twenty miles from where Marshal Soult was laying siege at Badajoz. The countryside would be swarming with French. Who the devil was this English lord his cousin must wed?

There could be little doubt who and what the viscount was. Rumors of British agents supplying information were always prevalent. All the more reason Victoria must marry the man before he left, since his destination could assure he might never return.

A warm hand came to rest on the captain's arm and he looked down to see Ines gazing at him with concern. "*Meu caro, Carlos,* do not worry about the Lady Victoria. This English *visconde* is a gentleman. He will do his duty to the young lady."

His Portuguese wasn't very good, but the captain was certain that the lady had just called him "my dear Charles." He felt a warmth filling him, then he glanced out the window as he remembered his cousin. There had been hundreds of times during his years at Stoneleigh he'd wanted to box her ears, but never so much as at this moment. Her headstrong nature would cost her dearly this time.

Charles could see Ridgecrest and Vic facing one another on opposite ends of the terrace like two knights about to engage in a joust. The captain knew he'd best find a vicar before Vic took it in to her head to run her future husband through with whatever came to hand. He felt sorry for the viscount, because the poor fellow had only a small inkling of the obstinate nature of the woman he was about to wed.

Charles swore softly. "Where the devil am I going to find a proper clergyman here in Portugal to marry them? You've got priests as thick as fleas on a dog's back, but only an English bishop can do the job legal and uncontestable."

"Bishop? Why, I believe there is a bishop who visits with my friend the Condessa de la Meda in Sintra. Is he your proper clergyman?"

"None more proper than the archbishop himself. We must leave at once."

Dona Ines looked toward the pair on the terrace. "I think it best I remain here. You will need space in the carriage."

Charles smiled down at the lady who'd captured his heart. "You are wise as well as kind, my dear. I'll need a bit of time to explain the circumstances. If not, I fear we'll scandalize this poor fellow to such a degree he won't be able to perform the ceremony. With both of them wearing breeches he might have difficulty determining which is the bride."

The senhora smiled, then quickly gave the captain directions to the condessa's villa. Charles took one last glance at his cousin to make certain she was behaving herself for the moment, before he hurried to his carriage.

On the terrace, Kit found that part of his anger had faded as he stood watching the outraged figure pace in the ill-fitting clothes. He pondered that he could overcome his anger so easily then realized that over the course of his journey he'd come to like his young companion. He wondered what had driven her to the extreme measure of fleeing to her cousin in Lisbon, a mere childish prank or something truly serious? But did it really matter after all? She had come and altered both their lives forever. He didn't have the time to ponder the implications. He must wed her quickly and be on his way.

Just for a moment, he tried to imagine her dressed in a gown with her hair properly done, but the image refused to come. She still looked very much the valet in her old-fashioned frock coat and breeches, her brown curls cut short and tousled by the wind. Not exactly a woman to fill a man with passion in her present rig.

He gave himself a mental shake. He couldn't delay settling matters. He moved across the flagstones and stood beside her. She watched him warily as he approached, defiance evident on her pale face. It was a countenance that held a hint of beauty despite the ravages of her strong emotions.

He was still amazed that he hadn't seen through the disguise. She had a full sensual mouth and porcelain skin, but he'd attributed those delicate features as boyish youth. He supposed it was because he'd been unusually distracted, his thoughts elsewhere much of the trip. Remembering his dangerous mission, he knew he must marry her before he left for the frontier.

"Lady Victoria, we must marry without delay." He put up his hand to stop her protest. In a tone that brooked no argument, he continued, "I won't allow you to leave this inn until we have said our vows."

"Who are you to be ordering me about, sir?"

Kit realized that sweet words would fall on deaf ears with the headstrong miss, so he decided to shame the lady into compliance. "I am the man whose act of kindness to a young boy has been repaid with

ungrateful defiance by the very same person who is
in fact a female."

Lady Victoria's cheeks flamed pink. "But I never
intended matters to take—"

"I know you meant no harm, but will you not be
held accountable for your foolish actions? Is there
no such thing as a female having honour and doing
what you know to be proper?" Kit held his breath
that he'd gotten to the lady's pride.

Her back straightened at the implied insult. His
very words gave her little choice if she were to keep
her dignity. Her searching gaze seemed to take his
measure. She stared at him for so long, he began to
doubt he'd gotten through to her then she gave a
soft sigh, and nodded her head in agreement.

Kit felt no joy at getting her acquiescence. The last
thing he needed was a wife, but he must protect this
woman's name. "Very well, after we are wed I fear I
must leave you in your cousin's care. The reason I
came to Portugal is important, and I cannot ignore
the matter. I shall instruct Captain Rydal to put you
on the first available ship back to Portsmouth, with
a proper companion and wardrobe. From there go
to my estate, Harwick Hall, near Farnham where my
mother and sister reside."

Her green eyes clouded with doubt at the wisdom
of his plan. "Can I not remain in Lisbon with Charles
until you return? It would be quite awkward meeting
your family without you."

"It's not safe for you to remain here." Kit knew if
his enemies got wind the English Phantom had a wife
in Lisbon, she'd be in grave danger. "I want you to
return to Farnham. Your cousin will be returning to
his unit and you would be alone in a foreign land."

He was struck with an idea on how to ease her

resistance about going into a strange household. "In truth, you could be a great deal of help to my mother. She finds managing the house a burden."

He noted a spark of interest in his future wife's eyes. "My lord, would you or your mother have any objection to my taking over management of your home?"

Despite the situation, Kit found himself half amused. The lady had shown little curiosity in his merits as a husband, but the idea of running his household held genuine allure. Then he remembered her cousin had mentioned the loss of her own former home, no doubt entailed away to some male relative. A female's lot was never easy. Did not every woman long for a home of her own?

"It would be expected of my wife. I think I can state as a certainty that my mother will be delighted to have a daughter-in-law willing to handle the domestic matters." On a reckless impulse, he bent and kissed her hand. "Will you do as I ask?"

Victoria's heart jolted when his lips touched the bare skin of her hand. A strange tingling raced up her arm and radiated through her. She knew she mustn't read too much into the gesture. Considering that her foolish actions had hurled them into a marriage of necessity, he was a true gentleman who was only being magnanimous. Could she be anything less? Taking a steadying breath, she said, "Then, my lord, I do consent to marry you and I shall journey to Harwick Hall without delay."

The viscount raised his head, and she stared into his eyes, but was disappointed. There was no look of the lover in his gaze, only resignation that their lives would forever be intertwined.

Just then, Dona Ines hurried onto the terrace car-

rying her cape. "I must apologize for interrupting
you, my lord, but Carlos's carriage will soon return.
Lady Victoria, perhaps you would wish to disguise
your attire from the clergyman, no?"

Victoria looked down at her clothes and nodded.
"You are very kind, Senhora de le Coelho."

Before the ladies left the terrace, Kit urged them
to take their time for he would need to speak with
the parson once the gentleman arrived. He strode
back into the room and summoned the landlord,
making certain arrangements for after the ceremony,
then he settled down to await the clergyman and the
captain.

Some twenty minutes passed before Captain Rydal
entered the parlour slowly, a questioning look on his
face. Kit gave only the briefest of affirmative nods,
and the soldier's face relaxed with relief. He then
entered the chamber and introduced the gentleman
who followed as the Right Reverend Nigel Boyce,
Lord Bishop of Cumberland, in Lisbon to visit his
wounded brother Colonel Maxwell Boyce.

The tall thin man wore a pair of thick glasses on
a large bulbous nose. He was a rather prosing fellow,
and quickly informed the viscount that they would
be breaking the rules by performing a marriage on
such short notice, but since the lady lived in his district
and the captain had informed him of the unusual
circumstances, he would officiate.

Kit graciously thanked the bishop, then ordered
refreshments while they awaited the bride. With a
slight jerk of his head, Charles indicated he desired
to speak with Kit alone. The two men moved to a
corner of the parlour as the bishop enjoyed a glass
of Madeira.

The captain cleared his throat nervously. "My lord,

I feel that since my cousin has tumbled you into this unforeseen predicament, I should lay all the cards on the table, so to speak. There is the matter of settlements."

Kit sighed, suspecting that what the captain would tell him was not good. "Settlements, sir? I think it is a mute point under the circumstances."

The captain's face took on a sheepish look. "Right you are, my lord. Just didn't want there to be any false assumptions on your part about Vic, er, I mean Lady Victoria."

Kit shrugged, his mind too preoccupied with the momentous step he was about to take to pay much heed to anything else. "What assumptions?"

"Didn't want you to think that Victoria, as the daughter of an earl, was an heiress. There's an estate near Carlisle, but it's entailed on the old earl's brother. By the time Uncle Gilbert died, he'd long been punting on the River Tick. Ran through what he'd inherited plus what Victoria's mother brought to the marriage."

Kit didn't know what to say. Money would never have been a consideration had he chosen to marry, still—he put the thought from his mind. He would do his duty and marry Lady Victoria, for better or worse. Kit's voice held a hint of bitterness, when he replied, "So her father ruined her chances on the Marriage Mart."

Charles stiffened. "My lord, I'll have you know that any gentleman should feel lucky to have Lady Victoria as wife. I don't know why she came to Lisbon, but you can be certain it wasn't on a whim. She has more good sense than half the officers of my acquaintance. The chit is a bit full of frisk, but I'd trust my home and hearth to her . . . that is if I had one."

"Captain Rydal, I am certain the lady is most worthy. You need have no fear I would treat her ill."

The soldier relaxed, his voice filled with a hint of apology. "I didn't mean to imply, er, I'm certain you will be an estimable husband. Only know that Vic ain't looking her best just now, dressed like some disreputable footman."

"Then I would have your promise that she is properly attired before she returns to England to my estate. It is my wish that she not remain in Lisbon. Just in case I don't return . . ." Kit pulled a small pouch of money from his pocket and pressed it into the captain's hand.

Charles nodded his head, knowing immediately what Lord Ridgecrest meant. War was a dangerous business, it was very possible that neither of them would return from their respective occupations.

At that moment, Lady Victoria entered the room. Kit had nothing to be ashamed of in his future wife. Dona Ines had transformed Victor Woods into Lady Victoria Woodley. Her brown hair had been swept away from her face and hidden beneath Dona Ines's black lace scarf which highlighted the soft glow of the girl's porcelain skin. The masculine clothing was completely concealed beneath the senhora's dark velvet cape. The widow had placed an artificial red rose behind Victoria's left ear, giving her a fragile look of vulnerability. For the first time Kit thought the lady looked, he paused for the proper word . . . temptingly appealing. Well, sort of . . . a little.

Yielding to his fate, he extended his hand to her. No doubt they would muddle through as did most married couples. Lord Ridgecrest and Lady Victoria Woodley faced the bishop and he began the ceremony.

* * *

A chill breeze swirled around Victoria as she stood
on the terrace of the Blue Flowers Inn watching the
sun sink in the western sky. She drew the senhora's
velvet cape tighter around her, but the coldness went
deep into her soul. Her mind still reeled at the idea
that she was married and to a near stranger.

She could hear Lord Ridgecrest speaking with
Charles and Dona Ines in the parlour where a simple
wedding feast had been laid out after the quick ceremony. She'd escaped to the terrace after the bishop
departed, needing some time to understand the turn
of events.

Neither she nor her new husband had partaken
much of the unusual Portuguese meal consisting of
sopa de feijão, a bean soup and *cabrito assado,* roast kid
with potatoes and peppers in wine and garlic. Under
different circumstances, Victoria knew she would
have enjoyed the exotic fare, but she had no appetite.

Before the meal, the viscount had requested paper
and pen, declaring the need to write several letters
which he wished Victoria to deliver on her return to
England. She'd attempted to make strained conversation with her cousin, but had been relieved when
Lord Ridgecrest had finished and they sat down to
dine.

Never in her wildest dreams had she suspected that
she would be returning to England a bride. She
couldn't truly think of herself as a wife just yet. They
weren't strangers to one another after their journey
together, but Victoria knew she didn't know him as
a woman should know the man she'd married. In
truth, that was not likely to change with Ridgecrest
leaving the inn this very night. She was filled with

conflicting emotions. He was her husband, but she wasn't yet ready for the intimacy the word implied. Not that he didn't stir something deep within her, but she knew he saw her merely a burden in his life.

A footfall interrupted her deep thoughts and she looked up to see her husband. "My lord."

"Shall we dispense with the formality, Victoria? After all, we are married. My friends call me Kit."

Victoria's pulse raced at his nearness, but she kept her voice calm. "As you wish, Kit."

He turned and looked out at the harbor as the shadows of the anchored ships were growing long. "Since you are my wife, I must be honest with you. My work here in Portugal is secret. My family knows I work for the government but they do not know the nature of what I do. You mustn't tell my mother or sister any of the details of our meeting or our marriage. If they ask, say we met in London and were wed there."

A flicker of uncertainty swept through Victoria. The man she'd married was in Portugal, not to visit his family as she'd so naïvely assumed, but on the deadly serious business of war. She wanted to ask a thousand questions, but she sensed this was not something he would tell a stranger, even one he had given his name. Determined not to add to his burdens, she squared her shoulders. "I will go to Harwick Hall and your secret is safe with me. But how do I explain your absence upon my arrival?"

Kit drew his gaze from the sunset to look at his new wife. There was a pensive shimmer in the shadow of her fine green eyes. Clearly she didn't know what to make of him or the strange new life she'd tumbled into. They would both have a great deal to adjust to over the coming months.

But that would come later, on his return to his home. He drew the two sealed letters from his pocket and handed them to Victoria. One was directed to his solicitor, informing him of Kit's marriage and requesting that an announcement be sent to the papers, the other was for his mother, spinning the same tale he'd encouraged Victoria to tell. There could be little doubt his mother wouldn't be pleased with the suddenness of his marriage, despite the fact she'd bedeviled him to wed. She wouldn't have expected him to chose a dowerless bride. In the missive, he'd also admonished the dowager to make his wife feel welcome, yet one could never be certain what to expect from his unpredictable parent.

"I've explained to my mother that I shall be working in York then traveling around England. That should account for the fact that I couldn't return to Farnham with you. I apologize for throwing you into the lion's den alone, as it were."

Victoria's expressive eyes grew tense. "Can I not journey to London and remain there until you return? I should enjoy that, having never been in Town before."

Kit cursed his loose tongue for such a blunder. Her flight to Lisbon showed a rashness of nature which didn't bode well for his peace of mind. The last thing he needed was to have a headstrong wife on the Town without someone to properly watch over her. He wanted her under the watchful eye of Jose, who managed to keep things generally in hand during Kit's absences. But Victoria was nothing like his sister and mother. Ordering the lady home might be a waste of his breath. On impulse he taunted, "Afraid to meet my family, my dear?"

The lady shot him a withering stare. "Certainly not.

If it is your wish, I shall return to Harwick and take up my household duties at once.''

Kit was satisfied that she would be safely situated at his home estate where there was little mischief she could get into until his return. "Very good, my dear. Then I shall bid you a good journey and farewell."

The gentleman turned, about to walk away from Victoria. She was suddenly overwhelmed with fear that she might never again see him. "My lord, er, Kit."

She didn't know what to say as he stopped and looked down at her inquiringly. After a moment of silence, he lifted her chin. "Don't look so forlorn, Victoria. No doubt we shall rub along well enough together." He learned down and brushed her lips with a soft kiss, then turned and left without a backward glance.

Victoria fingered her lips, savoring the memory of her first kiss. She prayed that God would return her husband safely to England.

CHAPTER FIVE

Rain pelted Kit as his horse pranced through the muddy street of Campo Mayor, the Arabian scarcely showing fatigue at the two days of hard riding that had brought them to the frontier of Portugal. He was bone weary, but he'd had to push onward to make tonight's rendezvous. He'd circled the small village and entered from the east after seeing nothing to arouse his suspicions of a trap. Still, he couldn't shake a feeling of impending disaster. It had nagged him since leaving Lisbon.

He attributed his dark mood to guilt over leaving the woman he'd just married. He tried to concentrate on the dangerous business ahead, but those expressive green eyes seemed to haunt his soul. It had only been a short time since he'd left Victoria in the capable hands of her cousin, but Kit wished he'd been able to see her on board a ship and safely on her way to Harwick. Marriage had made her his responsibility.

A dark figure scurried across his path and he

became alert to his surroundings. The hairs on the back of his neck prickled, then the person disappeared down an alley. No doubt it was some local returning home from an inn. He looked up and down the street, then realized he'd come to the small tavern where he was to meet Sir James.

A swinging sign proclaimed in Portuguese the run-down establishment to be The Brown Hen. The building was the largest of the surrounding structures, yet was still small by English standards. Kit tied his horse to a small leafless tree in front of the tavern.

He entered a low-ceilinged, smoke-hazed room which had crude plank tables scattered in front of a stone fireplace. What struck him was not the number of people present in the tavern, but the lack of loud noise one would expect from a gathering of that size. Low murmurs of conversation halted as he stood surveying the room. Something wasn't right.

With a nonchalance he was far from feeling, he drew off his oilskin coat and found an empty table near the fireplace, all the while looking for the man he'd come to meet. What he saw made his blood run cold. This was no collection of Portuguese farmers. Everyone in the room wore heavy wool greatcoats or long driving capes, which no farmer in such a remote village could afford. Unless he missed his guess, he'd walked into a room of Frenchmen.

It was a trap. The question was, could he bluff his way out of there? Had Marks already been caught? Had the so-called plot against Wellington been a mere ruse to draw out a few British agents, or only the English Phantom?

A wizened old man came nervously to the table, and Kit ordered a meal and wine in Portuguese. In an effort to maintain his cover he inquired if there

were any pigs or sheep for sale in the village. He saw
the tavern owner's gaze cut to a point somewhere
behind where Kit sat then the fellow shook his head,
before hurrying to the kitchen. A young maid scurried
in with a carafe of wine, a bowl of vegetable soup
and thick slices of bread, then hurried away, never
glancing at any of the other men in the room.

Hunger was no part of Kit's discomfort. He tried
to appear unconcerned as he spooned up the soup.
The meal was well prepared, but he didn't taste a
thing, he was so alert to what was happening around
him.

A voice behind Kit spoke in accented English. "You
speak the local language very well—for an Englishman."

Kit poured out a measure of the wine, ignoring the
man. He had to maintain his guise. He pretended
not to understand as he drank, then continued to
eat.

The man who'd spoken came to Kit's table, staring
down at him. The green jacket often worn by French
colonels was barely visible through the opening of
his grey cape. "Must I shoot you to get you to respond,
sir?"

Kit laid down his spoon and found himself staring
into a pair of cold blue eyes. This man was no fool.
Kit knew he mustn't make a single mistake. "*Por favor,
senhor. Não falo inglês.*"

The Frenchman gave a mirthless laugh and called
to one of his men, still speaking English. "He says
he speaks no English, Anton, but I wonder if he will
understand this. Shoot this British spy in the back."

Kit gave not a hint that he understood that he might
die within the next few minutes. Instead he grinned
then pointed at the colonel's uniform, switching to

a bad rendition of French. "Ah, sir, you are with Marshal Soult's army. I too work for the general. Have you seen any pigs or sheep?"

The Frenchman frowned, but switched back to his native tongue. "I know nothing of pigs except the ones that wear redcoats."

Pretending to laugh with the others, Kit nodded. "I am looking for real pigs, Colonel. The farmers hide them when they know you French are near. That is why your general pays me, Don Paulo Lorenzo, to seek them out."

Colonel Henri Dubois eyed the man before him with doubt. He'd been sent to intercept two British agents who'd been lured to this Godforsaken inn. French spies in London had warned of the network of men working out of Horse Guards, but they'd been able to find the name of only one of the agents despite their best efforts. The Frenchman only knew that two strangers would come to the tavern today.

The mission wasn't going as smooth as Dubois had planned. His unit had wounded the other agent from whom he could get no information. Was this the other spy seated before him, or was he working for Marshal Soult, reconnoitering for food for the army laying siege at Badajoz? Or was it *le Fantôme Anglais* that had proven so elusive? The man spoke flawless Portuguese, but then Dubois did as well, having an ear for languages. So that was no real measure of the man.

The colonel scanned the stranger's face, noting that this one looked different from the other. The dark hair and eyes, the olive skin looked native. He might well be some local man out to make money on this war that had invaded his land. The stranger had spoken the truth about the Portuguese and Spanish hiding their provisions and animals from the

French, knowing that Napoleon's army lived on the land, taking what they needed to survive. It was possible he was what he claimed to be.

But Dubois wouldn't risk losing a spy. "I apologize, but I must detain you for a few days, Monsieur Lorenzo. In the morning, I shall send a messenger to Badajoz and if the field marshal verifies your employment, you will be released unharmed to continue your search for pigs." Turning to one of the other soldiers, the colonel added, "Put him in with the Englishman."

Kit protested loudly in Portuguese before being led upstairs, then allowed himself to be pushed into a small dark room. In the light of a guttering candle he could see a body stretched out on a small bed. There was a soft rasping sound as the man drew breath. There was little doubt he was dying.

Kit bent and touched Marks's forehead. He was burning with fever. His eyes flew open but seemed not to focus on anything.

"James, it's Kit."

Marks attempted a smile which turned into a grimace of pain. "Kit, I was hoping . . . you'd get away from that French devil."

"Don't speak." Kit saw a jug of water had been placed on a small table beside the candle. He poured some into a cup and lifted the baronet's head to help him drink.

After sipping only a little, Sir James pushed the cup away. "It was all a trap, Kit. You've got to . . . get away. Tell Horse . . . Guards . . ." The man struggled for breath. "Kit, tell 'em the French have someone in . . . London's trying to . . . trying to get the names of our agents. Overheard the colonel sayin' so. P-promise me you'll get whoever it is." The injured man clutched at Kit's coat.

"I promise I'll find the man who betrayed us, James."

The baronet's face relaxed on hearing the words. He gave a soft sigh, then his head sank to the side as he breathed his last.

Kit bowed his head for a moment. He knew that he was destined for a similar fate as Sir James once the messenger returned from Badajoz, since spies were summarily shot. He had to get away. He rose and began to search for a way out of the airless room. He discovered on the opposite wall a shuttered window which had been nailed shut.

He was just barely able to get his fingers around the edge of the shutter. After several tugs, the aging wood splintered and came free, leaving his hands scraped and bloody but he paid little heed.

Kit looked out the opening to find the ground lay two stories below. He prayed the rain had softened the dirt into mud enough that he wouldn't break his ankle. Such an injury would seal his fate. He suddenly thought of his new wife, Victoria. He'd entered the marriage out of duty, but he knew in that moment when death might be an instant away that he wanted to go back to Harwick Hall. He wanted to be a husband and father. He wanted to live.

With one last glance at his late friend, Kit silently promised to get to London and find the person who was trying to destroy the network. Then he would go home and settle down, hopefully to build a life with the woman he'd married.

After climbing through the window, Kit jumped. He hit the ground and rolled before coming back on his feet unharmed. The cold rain and mud soaked his clothes, but he didn't care, he was free. He could see his horse still tied near the front of The Brown Hen, but he knew he'd be seen by the men in the tavern if he used the animal.

A shout sounded from upstairs and a man's head appeared at the small window. Kit dashed for his horse, knowing he'd been discovered. He was on the animal in seconds, kicking the gelding into a mad gallop, but men were pouring out of the tavern's front door.

A volley of shots sounded behind him. Kit felt only a stab of pain in his side. He'd been hit, but still he rode hard away from Campo Mayor.

Darkness soon swallowed the horse and rider as they made their way into the hills. Numb from pain and the cold, Kit kept pushing onward, north toward the Tagus River. Uncertain how much time had passed, he hoped he'd lost any pursuers but he knew he had to find shelter to rest or he wouldn't survive.

He came upon a small cottage in the hills. There was a risk that whoever lived there might turn him in for gold, but Kit knew he could go no further that night. He rapped on the door and an old man looked out, an ancient blunderbuss in his hand.

Kit claimed he'd been shot by a passing French patrol and begged shelter before he collapsed. The old man cursed the French, then called for the help of his wife to bring the stranger into his home.

Fortune smiled on the British agent that night. The couple was willing to take him in. The old man and his wife were alone, their only son having been killed by the French while trying to prevent marauding soldiers from stealing their only cow and a few goats.

The possibility existed that he might fall ill, or worse, die that very night. With that though in mind,

Kit insisted on writing a letter at once. He'd been on the verge of collapse by the time he finished the important missive. His last conscious breath was to beg the old man to see the message got to Father Curtis at the university in Salamanca.

Senhor Garcia took the letter as he'd promised, while his wife stayed and tended the stranger's wound. Within the week the senhor had returned and he aided his wife as she diligently nursed the Englishman over the course of the weeks he lay desperately ill. They were curious about the man who'd spoken like a native of Portugal. His feverish ravings were always in a mixture of Portuguese and English about his need to find a French spy and returning to a lady with green eyes.

The post chaise and four rolled through a set of gates where one of the two stone figures, Victoria thought they were angels, had toppled to the ground. The crumbled masonry had lain so long in the dirt, that ivy had grown up over the fallen sculpture.

While the young lady's face was a model of composure and dignity, her insides tingled with turmoil and curiosity about her welcome to Harwick Hall. She could scarcely believe that only two weeks ago she'd been in Lisbon and now she was entering the gates of her new home.

Despite Charles's protest, Victoria's stay in the Portuguese capital had extended to a full week in the company of the delightful Dona Ines. The senhora had persuaded *Carlos* he simply couldn't allow his cousin to return to her new in-laws without proper apparel. With a loan from her reluctant relative Victoria began the process of again becoming a genteel lady.

A young Frenchwoman who'd remained behind after Marshal Junot's retreat from Lisbon and just starting a millinery business, had, for a fee, speedily produced a traveling gown and several day dresses for Victoria. Hardly a full wardrobe, but the young lady promised herself a visit to London to properly outfit herself at some later date. She was feminine enough to want to look her best before her new husband again saw her.

The senhora's maid had provided a foul-smelling solution, the contents of which she refused to reveal, to strip the brown henna from Victoria's hair. Dona Ines had declared her ravishing when the fiery colour was again revealed. While Victoria would have far rather had the dark locks of her hostess, she was merely content to once again feel herself.

All during her transformation, she wondered where Kit was at that moment. Was he safe? Might he return before she left Lisbon and accompany her home? Despite her wish to again see her husband, she was doomed for disappointment. Kit hadn't reappeared by the day she embarked for England.

Captain Rydal had found a widow returning to England to accompany his cousin to Portsmouth. With a number of admonishments, he put the young lady on the ship and prayed she would do as her new husband had requested, but knowing that Victoria very often followed her own path.

Unlike the initial voyage, the return to England had been speedy and uneventful, on a small schooner, taking barely five days.

Victoria parted from her traveling companion after the arrival of her maid and footman, Betty and Theo, whom she'd sent a carriage for at once. They'd been full of tales of the uproar at the manor after her disappearance, but despite days of searching, Lord Stonebridge had returned home in a vile temper, which had nearly subsided until her letter informing him of her marriage had sent him into a new paroxysm of rage. They'd been only too delighted to leave the ranting earl's employ.

With proper servants and a modest wardrobe, the bride was now ready to meet her in-laws. As the carriage bowled up the drive, Victoria was nervous about what her reception would be. She fingered the letter from Kit to his mother through the fabric of her reticule. What had he told his parent about her and their sudden marriage?

Her mind drifted back to the kiss on the terrace in Portugal. It had been utterly sweet and enchanting. That simple embrace had left her wanting far more than just a secure home from his lordship. She longed for him to return to truly take her in his arms and whisper—

"Jingle-brained is what you are." Betty peered ahead at the shabby house they approached. "To marry a man you know nothing about. Why, the place looks haunted, my lady."

Victoria, jarred from her woolgathering, gazed at Harwick Hall which now loomed in the front window of the chaise. It was a huge Jacobean structure which had seen better times. Rows of symmetrical grime-covered windows lined the three stories. The ancient grey stone was mottled with shades of green and black blotches of mold and dirt, giving the house an abandoned appearance. A decorative balustrade which trimmed the roof was broken in several places. Still, the house had potential, or, Victoria thought, even a kind of archaic charm.

"Haunted? Don't be silly, Betty. Once all those windows are cleaned I'm certain you will soon be complaining of too much cheerful sunlight."

"I'll be complainin' all right, from an achin' back after cleanin' so many windowpanes."

The carriage drew to a halt and the postboy came to lower the stairs. As the women stepped down, Theo went to the door and knocked. They all waited for what seemed like ten minutes before the door opened but a crack and a white-haired maid with dirty apron and a cup of ale stared out at them. "What ye want? Lost are ye?"

Theo glanced at his mistress like she'd brought them to a mental asylum instead of their new home. "No, we are not, you old squeeze crab. Where's the butler? This is Lady Ridgecrest just arrived."

"Ain't got no butler, n'r footman, only old Jose an' me. And I ain't lettin' ye come in,' cause the real Lady Ridgecrest is in 'er parlour."

Victoria was dismayed. She'd come to a house of this size which had only one insolent maid and a man named Jose to run the entire establishment. If the servant's impertinence was an indication, it was clear that the dowager certainly had need of someone to take the Hall in hand.

Rallying, Victoria said, "We shall remedy the lack of servants in a trice. Now stand aside my good woman for I *am* Lord Ridgecrest's wife and I would meet the dowager and Miss Isabel Harden."

The old woman's brown eyes grew wide, then she shuffled back, opening the door. Victoria ordered Theo to pay the postboy and bring the trunks, then entered her new home. If she didn't know that some-

where deep in the manor, two ladies resided, she
would have sworn the house was abandoned. The
tables looked like it had been days since being dusted
and the long Oriental runner which ran the length
of the long narrow hall, looked as if the last detach-
ment of soldiers sent to the Peninsula had marched
straight through the house.

Within minutes the old servant ushered Victoria
and Betty into a rear parlour on the second floor. A
quick perusal of the lower floor rooms, as she'd
passed, left Victoria astonished. Faded drapes and
frayed furniture filled the house. Harwick was beg-
ging for someone who would love the old manor and
bring it back to its former glory. It was everything
she'd dreamed about after learning of her grandfather's legacy.

The maid's voice was full of doubt as she intoned,
"Says *she's* Lady Ridgecrest, ma'am."

Betty, who'd had enough of the insolent maid,
barked, "You are speaking of the Earl of Stonebridge's daughter, show some proper respect to Lady
Victoria."

The old servant just stared at the lady as if she'd
spied a spider on the rug, for she suddenly realized
that things were about to change at Harwick and to
her way of thinkin' it weren't goin' to be for the
better. Why, she might actually have to clean
somethin'.

The two women seated near the fireplace rose and
stared with bewilderment at the visitor. Victoria in
turn inspected her new relatives. The older lady was
short, dressed in black with Spanish lace draped over
her greying hair, an anxious look on her still handsome face. The younger one was tall and plump, her
raven black hair pulled severely away from her face

making it appear quite round. Her dress of dark grey wool with a white ruff at the throat was old-fashioned and unflattering to her large figure.

Isabel Harden smiled warmly at Victoria, as if she welcomed the rare event of company. Clasping her hands together, she said, "What a delightful surprise."

Victoria wasn't certain why, but she felt more in control of her life than ever before. She had the desire to make these women's lives more comfortable, if they would but allow her. Now all she had to do was win them over. She advanced on the ladies. "I do apologize for barging in this way without the least warning. I am Kit's wife. I hope you will call me Victoria."

"Wife?" The dowager parroted. "Kit is married?"

Seeing the dowager's face blanch white, Victoria reached out and took the lady's hands. "Pray, don't be distressed at this unsettling news of our wedding. I fear my father passed away but six months ago, thus a large wedding would have been unthinkable. Kit journeys to York even as we speak, but he wished to have all settled before he left, so we were married quietly. I hope you don't object to the suddenness of a new sister-in-law and daughter-in-law, Miss Harden, Lady Ridgecrest." Victoria felt only a twinge of guilt at the falsehood, for it would only worry both of Kit's relatives to know where he truly was.

Miss Harden came and took Victoria's other hand. "My brother is always one to do the unexpected. I can only say for myself I'm delighted to have a new sister." She leaned down and kissed her newly acquired relation, then gestured for Victoria to be seated, before she ordered Martha to show her ladyship's maid to a room in the servant's hall.

The dowager, once again seated beside the fire, eyed the visitor petulantly. "I should have known my son would never remember to invite us to his wedding. He would never think we might have enjoyed a visit to London, especially now that dreadful Cook has packed and run off."

"Run off?" Isabel snapped. "You drove her off with your constant complaints."

Victoria continued to listen as mother and daughter argued about the absent servant, seeming to forget about her. She was reminded of her parents' arguments. They were always worse when they'd been around one another for too long with no other company.

Victoria interrupted to give her mother-in-law Kit's letter. While the lady read the missive, Isabel gave her attention to her new sister-in-law.

"I must apologize for the state you find Harwick in, Lady Victoria." Isabel lowered her voice. "We have no visitors and so few servants, and Kit has done little to refurbish things. *Mamãe* has always said that Kit's wife could worry about such matters."

Music to Victoria's ears. "It's a challenge I shall gladly undertake."

"Did you hear that, *Mamãe?* Victoria wants to refurbish the Hall."

The dowager looked over the edge of the letter. "So, we are to be made uncomfortable with workmen and noise as well as constant rain and unfriendly neighbors. I told your late father how it would be." With a sigh, the lady dropped her gaze to the fire. "How I miss Portugal."

Isabel sank back in the chair, seemingly infected by her mother's melancholy. "As do I. There we had friends and parties and sunshine."

Victoria remembered that during the wedding supper Kit mentioned his family's sudden flight from Oporto four year earlier. She knew what it meant to give up everything you loved. Stoneleigh had been her life and now that was gone. But she'd not been faced with moving to a foreign country as well. No wonder these ladies sat here discontented and listless, quarreling with one another. Not only had they given up their beloved home and friends, but it seemed in the four years they'd been in England, they'd had little to replace their loss. Small tight-knit neighborhoods too often excluded outsiders, especially when they were foreign.

What the ladies needed were friends and entertainment. They'd obviously found little of that in Farnham. Victoria could think of no better place than London to find both.

The house would need a great deal of work. Once she had the requirements listed and the workmen hired, the bailiff could oversee the repairs. Perhaps the ladies would enjoy a visit to Town. Surely her husband wouldn't object to them going for, say a month, while the house was in complete disorder.

Isabel's dark eyes glittered with excitement after Victoria's plan was laid out. Miss Harden gazed thoughtfully at her new sister-in-law.

"I know I shouldn't ask, but I am curious. Are you . . . an heiress?"

"Isabel Harden, you forget yourself." The dowager's curious stare belied her harsh words to her daughter.

Victoria suddenly remembered that her own husband knew nothing of her legacy for she'd only informed Charles long after the viscount was gone.

With a laugh, Victoria said, "I'm delighted to say I am."

The three Harden ladies were all in fine fettle as they made their plans for a journey to London. Even Victoria's reminding them that they could only go after she'd settled matters about the house, did little to dim the ladies' enthusiasm for the proposed trip.

A warm May breeze carried the scent of wild thyme and primroses as Kit tooled the small hired gig along the drive to Harwick Hall. He wondered briefly if Horse Guards had managed to uncover the identity of the agent who'd cost Sir James his life and nearly cost Kit his. Senhora Garcia told him that her husband had ridden all the way to Salamanca and Father Curtis had promised to see the missive was sent on to London, but what had happened after that was a mystery for Lord Carew couldn't safely respond.

As Harwick came into view, Kit momentarily forgot about his trials in Portugal and was overwhelmed with a real sense of coming home for the first time. Then he looked askance at the old building. Something was different. He couldn't quite determine what it was, but the house was changed in some small way. Then he chuckled, thinking it was perhaps he who'd changed. He was now ready for the settled life of a gentleman.

Drawing his carriage up at the door, Kit jumped down and tied the reins to the bar above the splash board. While his gaze ran over the building he wondered how his sister and mother were getting along with his wife. A twinge of guilt surged through him that he'd abandoned Victoria to face his complaining relatives alone. He'd left his new bride without his support for over two long months, but it couldn't be helped. Unfortunately he needed to report to Horse Guards, and could only stay the night. Just long enough to see how everyone was faring before continuing to Town.

He tried the front door and found it unlocked. Stepping into the front hall, he was greeted by the smell of beeswax. A smile tipped his lips, for he was certain he had Victoria to thank for the polished condition of the entry. The woodwork gleamed as he'd never before seen it and there wasn't a single clod of dirt on the carpet.

There was no servant about, so Kit made his way up to his mother's favorite parlour. He opened the door and stopped dead on the threshold. The small dusty chamber had been transformed into an elegant little drawing room with rose curtains and matching floral wallpaper. Gone was the heavy worn furniture which had come with the house, and in its place was a cluster of simple satinwood sofas and chairs with rose damask covering.

The effect was a vast improvement, and Kit knew Victoria was behind the transformation, but his first thought was the expense. While the estate was unencumbered with mortgages, it wouldn't be for long, if his wife exceeded their income by lavishly refurbishing the house all at once. He would have to speak to Victoria about economizing until he'd made some needed improvements to the land which might produce more income.

The sound of hammering suddenly penetrated the viscount's bemused brain. He followed the noise and found himself in the High Great Chamber on the second floor. Several men were on scaffolds cleaning the relief which ran around the edge of the room.

A man was replacing a warped window facing and another was repairing the worm-eaten mantelpiece with an exact replica of the old one.

Amazed at the activity, Kit began to wander through the rooms. Some chambers looked completely refurbished while others looked like they were waiting their turn, as all the furniture had been covered or removed.

Kit continued his tour of the manor, hoping to find his wife, sister or mother. As he approached the kitchens, the sounds of voices raised his hopes that at last he would find the ladies.

Opening the door, Kit was stunned at the sight that met his eyes. Servants filled the large room, each busy with some task. There were maids darning linen, footmen polishing silver, and a new cook making bread. A man dressed in black, who looked very much like a butler, was seated at a table working on a household ledger.

Martha, spying his lordship, rose from a table where she was sorting herbs and curtsied. "Welcome 'ome, my lord."

Kit almost didn't recognize the woman with her pristine white apron, her white hair tucked neatly under a starched white cap. The room fell silent and the butler rose.

He hurried to Kit's side and bowed stiffly. "My lord, welcome home. I'm Bridges, sir. Is there some way I could be of assistance?"

"Bridges, I should very much like to speak to my wife."

"I fear, your lordship, the ladies left for London a fortnight ago."

Kit was dumbfounded. In his wildest imaginings he'd never expected to return to find his house swarming with workmen, men that he didn't know how he was going to pay, and his family gone to London. Where had Jose been to allow such an ill-advised journey?

"My valet, Senhor Rocha, is he here?"

The butler got a pained expression on his face. He made his opinion obvious about what he thought about pushing servants. "The man insisted that you would wish him to accompany the ladies, my lord. He is in London as well."

Anger began to build in Kit's stomach until it felt like a tight ball. He'd told his mother and Isabel they might go to Town next Season. He'd told Victoria not to go to London, yet she'd ignored him. All three had defied his wishes, but he knew where to lay the lion's share of the blame. His mother and sister would never have defied him, except for the interference of his willful wife. At least Jose was with them, but what good had the man been so far?

The butler, who'd been standing quietly surveying his new master, inquired, "Shall I send a footman to bring in your bags, my lord?"

"No, Bridges. Arrange for the gig to be returned to the King's Arms in Portmouth and have my curricle readied. I'm leaving for London as soon as you give me my family's direction."

The man announced that the ladies had leased Cranford House in Grosvenor Square, which only made Kit want to groan. No inexpensive residence for Victoria. She'd hired a huge town house. What the devil had he gotten himself into? Perhaps he should have asked more questions of the captain about his cousin.

When his curricle was at the door, he hurried to get on the road. He knew it was too late to worry about what he didn't know about his wife. What he did know was that he must get to London at once and take Victoria in hand before she sent him and his family to the poorhouse.

CHAPTER SIX

The journey from Farnham to Town could be driven in under five hours, but Kit's spirit had been far more willing than his healing body. He'd been forced to spend the night in Guilford, fatigue making his side throb.

Worries about how he would find funds to pay for the work already done at Harwick, plus Town expenses whirled in his head until near dawn. Also, there was still his promise to Sir James to unmask the spy which Kit fully intended to honour. His superior, Lord Carew, had few men available to mount such an operation in London. The sooner he got his family home to Harwick, the sooner he might aid in the hunt for the man who'd revealed Sir James's identity to the enemy. Feeling tired and ill-tempered, Lord Ridgecrest arrived in Grosvenor Square late in the afternoon the following day.

Traffic was light and there were few people about in the fashionable square, but at last Kit found a

passing lad to hold his team until a groom was summoned. The exasperated viscount stood taking in the
elegance of Cranford House. A strong desire to throttle his new bride welled up inside him. He would be
years recovering from the debt she'd plunged them
into and time was being lost that might cost another
agent his life.

Filled with a renewed sense of urgency, Kit lifted the
brass knocker. Within minutes, the butler, a rotund
fellow with a grey fringe around a bald pate, opened
the door.

"I am Lord Ridgecrest. Where is my wife?" Kit's
tone sounded excessively cross, even to him.

"I-in the ballroom, my lord."

Never one to abuse servants, Kit spoke more kindly.
"Pray, see that my cattle are taken to the mews, tip
the lad and have my bags brought in—" Kit waited
for the servant to respond.

"Matthews, sir."

"Thank you, Matthews, I shall find my wife on my
own."

"Very good, my lord." The butler took Kit's great-
coat, hat and gloves. He seemed relieved to part company from his irate employer.

Kit inspected the entry hall as the door closed
behind the departing servant. Everything was in the
first style of elegance from the black japanned tables
lining the walls to the Chinese vases which were filled
with hothouse flowers. All Kit could do was shake his
head and hope the house had come fully furnished
and staffed.

Kit discovered a library off the main foyer as he
peered through an open door. About to go on his
way to search for his wife, he paused. He needed to
inform Lord Carew of his arrival in Town. Eventually

there would be much to discuss. He entered the room and wrote a quick message to the earl informing the gentleman of his direction and his willingness to meet with his lordship as soon as was convenient. He went to ring for a footman, then heard Matthews directing someone to take Kit's trunk to the master's bed chamber. He gave the note to the butler, requesting it be taken to Horse Guards at once.

Music echoed in the hall. Someone with a passable skill was playing a waltz on a pianoforte. Kit followed the sound up a curved staircase. At the landing he faced double doors where the melody beckoned from behind the oaken barrier. He opened the door and his gaze was drawn to a lone couple who glided across the polished parquet floor.

Kit was baffled. The pair were strangers to him. He scarcely gave a passing glance to the gentleman because his gaze was drawn to the lady who waltzed round the floor.

The breath caught in his lungs. The unknown dancer was stunning. Her fiery red hair glistened with hints of gold as it caught the reflected light from the tall windows. It was cut short and barely covered by a scrap of white lace meant to be a cap. His gaze trailed down the slender white column of her arched neck to a provocative figure, encased in a willow green muslin morning gown trimmed with white ribbons. Kit's long-ignored passions stirred.

The rush of desire was immediately cooled by overwhelming guilt. He was wed—but not to a woman who warmed his blood like the one dancing before him. He pushed the unkind thought from his mind. Victoria no doubt would make a worthy wife once he got her spending habits under control.

Reluctantly drawing his gaze from the enchantress,

Kit scanned the room for the full figure of his wife. She was nowhere to be seen, but he found his sister standing beside the piano at which a pale young girl sat playing. Isabel was sorting through a box of sweetmeats, taking little interest in the dancing couple. He was struck by her changed appearance.

Essentially she was the same as she had been at Harwick, but her black hair was now fashionably styled with curls about her face. She wore a new simple pink gown which gave her skin a translucent glow. Just then she glanced up and, seeing her brother, she smiled with delight, tossing the uneaten treat back into the box. As she hurried towards him, he realized for the first time that she was quite pretty for a woman of such substantial dimensions.

"Kit, you are back at last. Victoria, *Mamãe*, and I had nearly given up hope that your business would be successfully concluded before summer."

A frail young girl at the pianoforte dropped her hands to her lap as she eyed the visitor with curiosity. When the music stopped so did the couple on the floor, but Kit consciously averted his eyes from his sister's ravishing guest, since the lady seemed to have cast a spell over him. Instead, he gave Isabel a kiss.

"You are looking lovely, dear sister."

"Oh, Kit, I am so nervous. We are invited to our first private party tomorrow evening at which there is to be dancing. What if the gentlemen do not ask me to take the floor? *Mamãe* says—" Isabel ceased her babbling, then blushed. "I forget my manners, allow me to introduce our guests."

While Kit and Isabel were greeting one another, Victoria stood frozen on the dance floor beside her partner. This was the moment she had been waiting for during the past two months—to see her husband again. Yet here he was and she was suddenly shy of him.

Then she realized that her sister-in-law was introducing the young baron with whom she'd been dancing. As the gentleman moved forward to shake Kit's hand, Victoria nervously followed, her mind full of questions. What would he think of her now that she was properly attired? Did he have an aversion to red hair like so many in Society? Had he been to Harwick? Was he angry to find them in London?

"Kit, may I present Lord Morton and his sister, Miss Jane Moore. Their mother was an old friend of Victoria's mother and she is hosting the party. Lord Morton has been so kind as to offer to teach us to dance the waltz, for it is all the crack you know. However, they tell me I cannot yet dance it at a ball. This is my brother, Christopher Harden, Viscount Ridgecrest."

The gentlemen exchanged formal bows and handshakes. Still Victoria waited for Kit to glance at her, but instead he again turned to his sister to inquire after their mother.

Isabel assured him that their parent was in remarkably good humor and enjoying her stay in London. Then a strained silence fell over the group. At last taking her courage in hand, Victoria said, "Welcome home, my lord."

His dark gaze flew to her face and he stared as if he'd never before seen her. Disappointment gripped her heart as a look of disbelief settled on his handsome countenance. Not exactly what she had hoped for.

Kit couldn't seem to comprehend what he was seeing. There were those engaging green eyes he remembered, but all else was changed. This couldn't be the Victoria he'd married, yet he knew it was. Suddenly realizing all eyes were on him, he stuttered out. "G-good afternoon, my dear."

Isabel, sensing some awkwardness between her brother and his new bride, suggested that she take the baron and his sister to tea with her mother while the newlyweds had a moment alone. She ushered their guests to the door.

Promising to join them in a few moments, Kit waited for the door to close behind the departing trio, thankful for the added moments to gather his thoughts about his wife.

This lady was an expert at surprising him, for he again felt an utter fool for not having recognized her. The blood throbbed in his loins as he realized that this desirable creature truly was the woman he'd wed in Portugal. His every instinct was to take her upstairs at that very moment, but he forced his rational self to the fore.

Despite her unexpected beauty, he reminded himself that this was the woman who'd turned his household upside down, throwing money in every direction but back in her reticule. He knew he must put an end to her free-spending ways, then get the ladies back to Harwick at once. He still worked for Lord Carew, and the French spy likely remained out there gathering information.

He drew his hands behind him for fear he might reach out to stroke her satin skin, but he still stared, marveling at her transformation. Angry with himself for the magnitude of desire she evoked when he'd meant to take her to task, he spoke more sharply than he intended. "Well, madam, what have you to say for yourself?"

Her delicate brown brows rose slightly. "Say, my

lord? Why, was your business in Portugal successfully concluded?"

"We shall not speak of Portugal. I refer, madam, to arriving at Harwick and finding the Hall at sixes and sevens, all manner of changes being enacted, my wife and family nowhere to be found."

Her expressive green eyes darkened. "How dare you criticize my actions when you expressly told me to take over the management of Harwick?"

"I meant you were to take over the household duties as any proper wife would. Not to set about expensive renovations with little thought to the consequences to the estate's income. And how do you justify dragging my mother and sister to London, spending money which the estate doesn't have for gowns, this house and heavens know what else."

His contemptuous tone sparked Victoria's anger and her green eyes glittered dangerously. "My lord, I successfully ran Stoneleigh Manor for two years for my ailing father, and felt myself fully able to handle the business of making Harwick more livable for your family. Forgive me if you think I overstepped my bounds. The journey to London was simply to spare your mother and sister the discomfort of living in the house during the worst of the restoration as well as some much deserved entertainment which seems to have been lacking in their lives." By now Victoria's tone had turned frigidly cold. "As to the matter of money, I can assure you that the Harwick estate has not been lessened by one farthing for the renovations or for this town house. Now, if you will excuse me, I will retire to my room for I am engaged to go to the theatre with Lord Morton and his sister."

Kit stared speechless as his wife, completely unrepentant for her rash and extravagant behavior, sailed out of the ballroom, slamming the door as she left. The sound echoed in the empty ballroom, bringing him out of his stunned trance.

Had he been out of line about her right to refurbish Harwick? After all she was his wife and he had told her to manage things. But what the devil did she mean about not having spent any of the estate's money? That was simply impossible.

All he was certain of was that she'd looked magnificent in her anger. The colour had risen in her porcelain cheeks and her sensual mouth had quivered with indignation as she'd glared back at him. He pushed the enticing imagine from his mind. He was more confused than ever. He needed to know what Victoria meant. No doubt his mother could tell him.

Kit felt foolish having to inquire about his wife's actions to another. He thought it ironic that both his sister and mother were better acquainted with Victoria than he was. When the image of her shapely curves floated up in his mind, he realized that was something he would be delighted to change. For now, he had to sort out this mess with her. From her reaction, he wasn't likely to be welcomed to his lady's bed anytime soon.

With that daunting thought in his mind, Kit set out to find his mother and see if she could unravel the mystery of the unspent money.

Anger kept Victoria's back rigid until she closed the door to her bedchamber. She sagged against the wood panel of the closed portal struggling not to cry, her anger was so great. Nothing had been as she'd envisioned upon Kit's return.

He hadn't made a single inquiry about how she'd

managed after he'd left her in Lisbon, nor praise at how she'd improved conditions at Harwick, not even a small compliment about her changed appearance. There were only bitter accusations about having over-stepped her bounds at the manor and her excessive spending, as if she were merely some hired servant. She should have explained about her legacy, and would have if he hadn't made such horrid accusations without giving her a chance.

A knock sounded on the door bringing Victoria's bitter musings to an end. She quickly moved to her dressing table. Struggling to get her temper under control, she called for the visitor to come in, then held her breath hoping it might be his lordship come to apologize. She was doomed to disappointment.

Betty entered the chamber, then halted as she eyed her mistress. Having served as maid to Lady Victoria since the young lady was fifteen, the servant knew her moods well. This one boded poorly for the newly arrived Lord Ridgecrest.

The serving girl had gotten a glimpse of the hand-some gentleman as he'd exited the ballroom. He'd enquired about his mother's whereabouts and she'd informed him the dowager was in the Green Drawing Room entertaining guests. He'd appeared—angry was too strong a word, testy was better. His words had been clipped, his mood distracted. Had the newly-weds quarreled so soon after being reunited?

Betty knew it was best to ignore the lady's foul mood, so she drifted to the wardrobe and began to inspect the gowns. "Are you still plannin' on goin' out now that his lordship's come home?"

Victoria straightened as she eyed her maid in the mirror. There was a defiant glimmer in her eyes when she said, "Of course. I cannot send regrets at so late an hour. I wish to wear the bronze sarsnet." She knew the new gown was flattering and she was determined to look her very best. Her husband might not appreciate her charms, but at least Lord Morton would.

She tugged her cap from her hair and began to brush the curls with vigor. No doubt, the viscount would be full of apology when he learned about her legacy and that his marriage had made him wealthy. Well, she would not forgive him so easily.

Kit stood by the window impatiently drinking his tea while Isabel and his mother entertained Lord Morton and his sister. He'd excused Victoria's absence to them, saying she was fatigued and had retired to her room. Etiquette demanded that he should withdraw to change his travel-stained clothing, but he was too anxious to speak with his mother to worry about such trifling matters.

The young baron had been full of concern upon hearing her ladyship was not to join them. Kit eyed the fashionable cub with a jealous eye. The man had been holding Kit's beautiful wife improperly close during the waltz to his way of thinking.

Under the viscount's hostile gaze, the Moores soon took their leave. Isabel threw her brother a livid glance for his discourteous behavior then walked their guests to the door. Lord Morton hesitantly inquired if the ladies still wished to go to the opera that evening and Miss Harden assured him they did. Promising to come round by eight, he and Miss Moore departed.

Isabel arrived back in the drawing room to hear her mother's angry voice. The lady had lapsed into Portuguese. "What has gotten into you, Christopher

Harden? Why, you were positively rude to that nice young man and his sister.''

Kit knew that his behavior had been unpardonable, but he was not in the mood to be distracted from the matter which he'd come to discuss. ''What has gotten into me? I return to Harwick after two months only to find that despite my wishes to the contrary, my family has gone to London.''

Isabel, who'd moved to stand behind her mother, didn't understand her brother's mood. ''But Victoria thought—''

Kit raised his hand to halt his sister's explanation. ''My wife was wrong. You will pack your trunks and be ready to leave London by the end of the week.''

''No.'' The word was said in unison by the ladies and echoed in the room like a cannon shot.

Kit stared in astonishment at not only his sister's but his mother's outright refusal to do as he wished. It was perhaps the first time they'd agreed on anything in the last four years, but then he laid the blame for their sudden disobedience to the one person who had the effrontery to interfere with their lives, Victoria.

The dowager set her empty teacup back on the tray, then peevishly said, ''We don't want to go back to Harwick. Things are quite different now.''

''Different? Because I have a wife?''

Isabel nodded. ''Not just a wife, but an heiress.''

''Heiress! Victoria! Where did you hear that Banbury tale?'' Kit stared at his sister, baffled. Captain Rydal had assured him his wife was penniless.

Isabel put her fists on her ample hips and bristled, '' 'Tis no tale. I was with her when she visited her grandfather's solicitor to arrange the lease on this house. She inherited fifty thousand pounds from a secret codicil in the late Lord Morrow's will. Did you not know?"

Kit was bereft of words. "I . . . that is . . . she never—"

A knock sounded on the door relieving the viscount from having to explain how he'd married a woman he knew so little about.

Matthews entered with a message on a tray which he extended to Kit. Breaking the seal, he read the letter requesting he come to Horse Guards at seven. He looked at the ormulu clock on the mantelpiece. There was scarcely an hour until his meeting. He would have to sort out the muddle with his wife later.

"There is urgent business I must attend."

Isabel came from behind her mother's chair, taking her brother's hands. "Please say that we might all stay in London. There are things to do and see. We have made friends. I promise not to tease you to take us to balls or the theatre. We shan't be pestering you for money because Victoria has seen fit to give both *Mamãe* and I an allowance." Seeing what seemed to be a refusal in his dark eyes, she proclaimed, "It is dreadfully lonely at Harwick and dear Victoria promised us a taste of the Season."

Kit looked down at the hands which clutched his so desperately. He realized this was important to his sister. When he looked up his gaze shifted to his mother, who sat anxiously awaiting his verdict. A surge of contrition coursed through him. He'd given little thought to what life had been like for his family, left continually alone at Harwick with no friends or family and little to occupy their days.

Should he allow his wealthy wife to pay for their visit to Town? He knew by law Victoria's fortune was deemed his, but somehow it seemed improper to take her money as his own considering the circumstance of the marriage. The very thought was abhorrent, but until he had the estate producing more, he couldn't afford to provide this level of comfort for his family.

Still, he had his mother and sister to consider. He wouldn't force them to return to Harwick against their wishes. He would just have to find a way to repay every cent to Victoria for her generosity.

"Very well. You may have your Season, Isabel."

The delighted miss threw her arms around Kit, nearly knocking him off his feet. She gave him a kiss. "You won't regret it, dear brother."

Kit wasn't so certain about that. If they hadn't captured the French agent, he would be embarking on a dangerous mission right here in Town, with his family in harm's way. It made him vulnerable. They could inadvertently become pawns in his dangerous game. He would have to think of a plan to keep them safe. "I have an appointment. I must change."

As he reached the door, his sister called, "We shall be at the King's Theatre with Lord Morton and Miss Moore this evening, if you should care to join us after you conclude your business."

After exiting the room, Kit paused in the hall outside the drawing room. He owed Victoria an apology. He detested the idea of living on his wife's inheritance. It smacked too much of him being a fortune hunter. Is that how she would see matters as well? The thought rankled. He would make it clear to her he would repay the money.

Kit summoned a servant to show him his room. He was led to a large chamber at the rear of the third floor. Jose was in the dressing room. A look somewhere between defiance and apology defined the old man's lined face as he unpacked the viscount's trunks.

The valet was fully prepared to defend his inability to stop the ladies' removal to London. He'd been impressed by the new viscountess's good sense and had fallen in with her wishes, but to his surprise, Lord Ridgecrest never mentioned the subject. He merely wished to change out of his travel-stained clothes. Clearly his mind was on other matters.

At last, dressed in an olive jacket with a grey striped waistcoat and grey pantaloons, Kit halted outside his wife's door, wondering what his reception would be after his unfair treatment of her. The least he could do was apologize before he went to his meeting. Fully prepared to face her ire, he knocked and was bade to enter.

Victoria sat before her dressing table donning a simple necklace of amber stones fashioned like flowers and linked by gold filigree. She wore a bronze evening gown which was cut low enough to expose a tantalizing hint of her white breasts. Heat rushed to his loins as he stood drinking in his wife's beauty, all thoughts of why he'd come momentarily gone. He didn't want to be anywhere but where he was at that exact moment.

"You wished something, my lord?" Green eyes glared at him, full of reproach.

Jarred from his trance by her cold tone, Kit straightened. "I believe I owe you an apology, Victoria."

She offered no comment, merely sat quietly waiting for him to continue. There was no softening of the expression on her pretty face.

His voice dropped lower, taking on a soft silky quality. "I should have given you a chance to explain about having run your family estate and about your legacy. Instead I was rude and overbearing."

Still the lady sat staring at him, making no attempt

to end the animosity between them. Realizing he
wanted to do more than give her empty words, he
came to stand beside her. There was a slight quiver
to her full lips as he drew near, making her look
utterly feminine and defenseless. He took her hand,
drawing her to her feet. He was filled with the need
to kiss away her fears about him, the marriage, or
both. Then the delicate scent of roses filled his senses
and he struggled to resist the urge to take complete
possession of his wife at that very moment. He
reminded himself she was young and innocent. He
had to take his time to woo this delectable creature
to his bed. With that in mind, he cupped her chin
with his hands.

"Forgive me for failing to tell you that you are
beautifully enchanting, my dear." Kit's mouth then
covered hers hungrily. Her tentative response was so
innocent and sweet, she stirred his desire as never
before. He wished he had the time to teach her all
he knew about kissing and more. With great effort
on his part, he drew away from her. Lord Carew was
waiting, and Kit cursed that fact at the moment. "I
fear I must leave, for I have been summoned to Horse
Guards."

Reluctantly Kit went towards the door, then he
looked back at Victoria. "My mother and sister have
begged that they might stay in London for the balance
of the Season. I have agreed you all may remain. I
would ask, however, that you keep a record of what
you spend and I shall repay you when I am able. I
hope you have an enjoyable evening."

The viscount closed the door, leaving Victoria with
her emotions in turmoil. She'd been determined not
to easily forgive his lordship's unpardonable behavior
in the ballroom. Then he'd been there looking exces-

sively handsome and he'd apologized then kissed her, leaving her breathless and wishing he would do it once again.

She'd been in alt. Here was the Kit she'd been waiting for, but his parting comment had been like a slap in the face. He wanted her to keep an account of the money she'd spent—like some hard-fisted banker, to be repaid like a common money-lender. Was this the way one treated a cherished wife? Not to Victoria's way of thinking.

She began to pace about the room, trying to sort out her conflicting thoughts. Despite their wedding vows, he still treated her like a stranger. He saw the legacy as her money, not theirs. She felt like a complete outsider.

But was he being so unreasonable. They were, after all, nearly strangers. Regardless of her attraction to Kit, she knew little about him other than what she'd learned from his mother and sister as well as their brief time as traveling companions. He knew less about her. For two weeks he'd known her only as a young man, two days as a woman. Perhaps she was being unfair to expect more from him so soon.

Victoria trailed her fingers over her lips, remembering the warmth of Kit's mouth pressed to hers. That soul-searing kiss made her desire more than marriage to a stranger. It also gave her a sense of hope. But did he want anything more than a marriage of convenience? One forced on him at that.

He'd given her proof enough with his kiss that he found her desirable, but had she touched his heart. She had no way of knowing for certain. What she did know was that until she was certain of his affections she'd never surrender to him.

CHAPTER SEVEN

Horse Guards, a large Palladian building beside Whitehall Palace, housed the Headquarters of Staff. The Depot of Military Knowledge, for whom Kit worked, was so small, so secret, and so under-funded by Parliament that it had been relegated to offices in the attic.

The Earl of Carew's appointment to head the small section had been a singularly wise choice by the Duke of York. A widower in his fifties, Carew had long ago lost interest in Society and its enticements. While the ladies and gentleman of the Beau Monde engaged in their nightly rounds of entertainments during the Season, his lordship was often found in his tiny berth deciphering messages or planing new campaigns for his stalwart band of British agents.

At present he was seated behind a cluttered desk too large for the small room, his head bowed over the notes from a retired Bow Street Runner the earl had hired with his own money to help discover a

French agent known to be in London. He looked up when the clock stuck seven, wondering what had happened to Lord Ridgecrest.

Some minutes later, the sounds of footsteps on the stairs made the earl rise in anticipation. After a brief knock, the door opened to reveal the viscount. The earl came round the desk to embrace the young man he'd come so close to losing in the last operation. It was a nightmare that haunted Carew. Too often he was sending these willing young men to their graves but he reminded himself that England's young men died every day on the battlefields in the Peninsula. It was one of the horrors of war.

Lord Carew thought the viscount looked a bit distracted, but he knew his brave lads had a difficult job. The hardest part was not telling their loved ones about their dangerous missions. "Christopher, you are looking well despite your ordeal."

"Thank you, my lord. Did you receive my letter from Lisbon?"

The gentlemen moved to take seats, having little time for the social amenities. "Scarcely a month ago, my boy. And I've been busy searching Town for this French blackguard." He picked up the bits of paper that had been torn from an Occurrence Book and handed them to Ridgecrest.

Kit scanned the writing, then his brows rose in surprise. "You think the informant is a woman?"

Lord Carew leaned back and spread his hands in a gesture of uncertainty. "I wouldn't have thought so, but Grafton, the Runner I hired to look into the matter, is convinced the lady is, if not our French spy, then the link to him."

"Is she an émigrée?"

The old man shook his head. "I've met the lady.

One meets her at all the fashionable affairs. Not a trace of an accent. Grafton can't find where she came from prior to arriving in Bath in the Autumn of '06. Married old Sir Hartsfield Frey the following spring and she brought him to Town and began to cut a swath through the local barracks, so to speak. Discreetly, I might add, because there was never a breath of scandal about the lady. Then two years ago Sir Hartsfield died and the lady disappeared, presumably in mourning, but within six months she was back, only this time with little interest in the gentlemen in regimentals.''

"And your Mr. Grafton thinks that suspicious?''

Lord Carew opened a drawer and drew out a sheet of paper. He pushed it across the desk at Kit. The white vellum had four names neatly inscribed in a list, a date after each. The final name written was Sir James Marks, followed by the day he died.

Kit looked back at the earl with a dawning realization.

"That's right, my boy. Former agents killed since the beautiful Lady Frey returned to London. Two of them found just outside Town.''

"A mere coincidence?''

"Grafton thinks each agent at some time was involved with the lady, but she was very circumspect. He could find no hard evidence to prove his theory. That's where I need your assistance, my boy.''

"You want me to work with your Runner to find the proof?''

Lord Carew chuckled. "Heavens, no. Grafton would quit in the blink of an eye, if I insulted his skills by foisting a young 'blade,' as he calls you lads, onto him. What I want you to do is seduce the information from Lady Frey.''

"Seduce?" Kit knew the only woman he was interested in seducing was the ravishing redhead under his own roof. How was he going to woo his wife to his bed if he was casting out lures to Lady Frey?

" 'Tis the only way to find the truth, my boy."

The earl was right, but still Kit's mind balked at the task. For the first time in the four years he'd worked for Lord Carew, Kit wanted to refuse his assignment. He wanted to get to know the woman he'd married, to truly live his life. Then he remembered that Sir James would never get that chance, and Lady Frey might be the reason.

He'd made a promise to the dying baronet in Portugal and honour demanded that he see it through. "I shall do as you wish, my lord."

"Wait two days before you make any move to make the lady's acquaintance. I want to see if she approaches you. We must learn her method of finding out who my agents are. If there are leaks of information we need to find them and plug them up."

Kit knew he was facing a difficult task. Clearly this lady, if she was a spy, was no fool. Her activities showed that she'd been successfully gathering information since England went to war against France.

Lord Carew rose and came round his desk. "Shall we go to my club and drink to your success with the widow, Christopher?"

Suddenly, he realized that to convince Lady Frey of his interest, he would have to convince the world that his was a marriage of convenience. He must keep Victoria at arm's length in the circles where Lady Frey moved. It was the last thing he wanted to do. For the first time, Kit cursed this life of subterfuge he'd chosen.

* * *

"Dickey, me hocks is near froze." Jimmy Brown
stomped his cold feet to make his point. "What we
doin' here?" The young pickpocket nervously stared
across the great expanse of ground which was the
Horse Guards Parade. For a lad who'd grown up in
the cramped spaces of London's slums, such wide
open spaces made him uncomfortable.

"Shut yer gob. I get business 'ere."

Jimmy snorted, knowing Dickey West had never
done a lick of honest work in his life. Not but what
the young file didn't admire his friend, for Dickey
was bang up to the mark in Jimmy's humble opinion,
always having some new plan for separating the nobs
from their blunt. But standing outside a building
filled with soldiers on an unseasonably cold May
night, wasn't Jimmy's idea of a wise plan. Still, he fell
quiet and waited to see what Dickey's lay was.

Finally two gentlemen appeared in the archway and
stopped between the two guards as the younger one
donned a black cape. Dickey snapped, "Stay put."
Then he hurried towards the men.

Jimmy stared with admiration as his friend barreled
into the gents, nearly knocking one off his feet. The
two guards hurried forward and there was a small
ruckus as the men tried to help Dickey stand and the
soldiers kept trying to get him to move along. Then
one of the guards jabbed at the young thief with the
end of his musket calling, "On your way, you thatch-
gallows." Dickey made a rude gesture and hurried
back to where Jimmy stood as the gents climbed into
a carriage and disappeared into the night.

"Did you spice one of the swells?" Jimmy's mouth
watered at the thought of the plump purse his friend

had lifted. There'd be a real meal at a tavern instead of dog's soup at the thieves' den where they usually slept in St. Giles.

"Are ye daft, boy? Wasn't goin' to nip off with a purse in front of two fellows with barkin' irons."

" 'Twas muskets not barkers."

"Don't matter, I'd be just as dead either way. Come on."

Jimmy was puzzled, but he followed his friend round the dimly lit square and down Parliament Street. The boy soon realized Dickey must have a plan for they made their way into the cobbled streets of Mayfair, always avoiding the Watch, instead of back to the narrow filthy alleys of St Giles.

At last they came to a house on a quiet street of houses. Jimmy was astonished when Dickey went up to the front door like he was a regular flash cull and knocked. Jimmy held back, but his friend motioned him forward. "Hold yer tongue and agree wit' what I says."

A skinny maid with pock-marked cheeks came to the door. Jimmy was amazed when she stepped back and seemed to welcome the likes of him and Dickey into the hall. "I'll see if the mistress can see you."

A toothy grin settled onto Jimmy's face as he surveyed the veritable treasure land before him. He reached out for a silver tray on a nearby table, but Dickey's strong hand clamped on his arm. "No pluckin' this goose, lad, or I'll skin ye alive."

Jimmy was beginning to think his friend had taken a knock to the brainbox or worse—gotten a dose of religion from that Methody parson what was always rantin' 'bout sin and lookin' for believers. All Jimmy knew was if Dickey stopped drinkin' and wenchin' and started preachin' they was partin' ways. Why he'd had two prime chances tonight for easy pickin's, and their pockets were still as empty as Jimmy's father's promises of easy riches for the life of a pickpocket.

The maid returned to usher the two street denizens into a small parlour. The elegantly furnished room had two occupants, a man who stood at the windows with his back to the visitors and a woman lying on a sofa before the fire.

At nine and twenty, Eve Frey looked like an angel. She was slender and blond with large expressive corn-flower blue eyes, full sensual lips and flawless pink cheeks. There was a delicacy about her that made men want to protect her, but the image was an illusion, for the lady had a will of iron. She'd lived a harder life than most and by the age of sixteen was a hardened veteran of the streets. Her mother was a French maid, her father the master of the house who tossed mother and child into the streets. Eve's mother had struggled for fifteen years to feed her young daughter. With her last dying breath she'd cursed Evette Beaulieux's English father.

Young Eve carried her mother's hatred of the English with her. Needing work, she had gone to Sommers Town, the place where most of the French émigrés resided in London, and she began to ply her trade on the street. It was there that she discovered a way to wreak her vengeance on the despised English with her encounter with René some seven years ear-lier.

She eyed the Frenchman with a touch of exaspera-tion, knowing he expected her to handle the interview with these ruffians. She dropped her satin-slippered feet to the floor and stood to face Dickey West.

"Who is that?" she demanded, pointing at Jimmy.

"Me partner. Takes a long time to watch a big place like the Guards. Jimmy 'ere was a big 'elp."

"And I suppose you expect me to pay him the same as you?" the lady sneered.

"Only seems proper, ma'am, what with all the work the lad's done fer me."

"Well, you hired him, you are responsible for paying him from your share. Have you a name for me?"

Dickey's face fell. His plan for doublin' his pay wasn't goin' just like he'd planned. "Well, er, 'tis Jimmy what's got the name."

"Then you are worth nothing to me. Get out." Eve was no fool.

Dickey shook his head sadly. "Jimmy don't speak to no one but me."

Eve stared at her informer thoughtfully. She walked to a small desk beside the thief and drew open a drawer. Before Dickey could move an inch she'd pulled a small blade from inside and pointed it straight at Dickey's throat. "I'll not be played with by the likes of you. Do you have a name for me or not?"

The frightened thief looked into the mort's eye and knew she was deadly serious. "Rigdecrest, ma'am. 'Is lordship called 'im, Ridgecrest."

Eve lowered the knife. "I think you are become more trouble than you are worth, Dickey." Replacing the weapon to the drawer, she pulled out a purse and gave him his reward.

Dickey stared at the coin. "But this ain't but 'alf of what ye owes me fer a name."

"True. I deducted half for all the trouble you have caused me tonight. Now be gone and don't return. Our business dealings are at an end."

Dickey shoved the coin into his pocket glaring at

the lady. He turned and motioned for his friend, then they exited the parlour.

At last the man at the window turned. In accented English he asked, "Was that wise, *mon petit*? How will you get the names we need?"

" 'Tis becoming too dangerous to continue this game, René. I think someone has been following me." Eve came and slipped into the man's arms. "Can we not leave for Paris? You promised. Forget about this Ridgecrest."

René grew still. "You have seen someone trailing you?"

Eve shook her head. "No, 'tis only a feeling I get at times."

The Frenchman laughed. "Women and their feelings." He tilted her chin upward. "Ridgecrest shall be our last one. If you are very good and use the perfect . . . inducement, he might tell us everything we want to know. Then we sail for France."

Eve threw her arms around René's neck and showered kisses on his face. Paris had always been her dream. She was confident in her prowess to seduce information from unsuspecting men. This Ridgecrest would be whispering his secrets in her ear soon if she had her way.

As René began to nibble at her neck, Eve decided she would instruct her man of business to quietly begin to sell off the contents of this house old Hartsfield had left her. There was no need to arrive in Paris a pauper. With that thought, she surrendered herself to the passion of her French lover.

She discovered later that due to her disagreement with Dickey, there was far less silver to sell. The young thief and his friend had taken everything that their hands touched as they'd exited Lady Frey's house.

The Harden town coach drew to a halt on Haymarket. Kit stepped down and hurried into the theatre in search of his family. He'd only lingered long enough for one drink with Lord Carew. The viscount had pleaded fatigue, but in truth he wanted to spend some small time with his new wife before he began his dark intrigue with Lady Frey.

The theatre foyer was filled with people and he quickly scanned the gathering, hoping to locate the ladies or Lord Morton, but they weren't to be seen. He'd just inquired about the direction of the baron's box from a nearby gentleman when he heard someone calling his name. He looked up to see Major Cooper winding his way through the crowd towards him.

"Kit, I'm delighted to see you back safe and sound." Edward lowered his voice. "I was at Horse Guards yesterday and heard from Lord Carew that all did not go well."

That was an understatement in Kit's view, but he didn't wish to discuss such secret affairs in a public place, so he merely nodded his head. "I'm surprised to see you still in England, Edward."

The major tapped his leg. "Damned thing wouldn't mend. Finally a surgeon reopened it last month and it's now healed, so I leave for Spain at the end of the week. Just got back from saying my farewells to my family in Essex. Speaking of family, I had the honour of making your cousin, Mr. Paul Harden's, acquaintance. Splendid fellow."

Kit hadn't thought of Paul Harden in ages. Being only distant relations, the cousins hadn't met until they'd both been sent to university. But the short-

lived friendship had come to an end when Paul's
father had died abruptly, requiring he return to
Chelmsford to run the family's holdings. Kit had
regretted that, for he'd liked his burly cousin excessively. "Was he in good health? Haven't seen him
since he left Oxford."

"Seemed in capital spirits." The major, seeing himself being signaled by a particularly pretty matron
with a rather scandalous reputation, quickly said his
good-byes.

Kit wished his departing friend a safe journey, then
made his way up to the third-floor balcony to find
Lord Morton's party. He entered the box and to his
surprise he discovered the small space overflowing
with gentlemen. On one side of the cubicle, his
mother, sister and Miss Moore were sitting in conversation with a young cub barely out of the schoolroom
and an older gentleman. Both seemed intent on flirt-
ing with the frail Miss Moore, a young lady with little
beauty but an excellent dowry. On the other side was
Victoria, looking ravishing as she sat amidst a crowd
of dashing young bucks which included Lord Morton.
That gentleman looked like a small dog trying to
guard a bone as he hovered at Victoria's side.

An urge to toss every one of the men who stood
there ogling his beautiful wife over the rail and into
the pits surged through Kit. Suppressing his more
violent tendencies, he politely greeted his mother
and sister, giving himself time to get control of his
temper, then he turned towards his wife and bowed.
"My dear Victoria, might I steal you from your admirers for a stroll in the hall before the intermission
ends?"

Several of the men made disgruntled noises, but
Kit merely ignored them and led his wife, who smiled

tentatively at him, into the hall. His senses were overwhelmed with the feel of her hand on his arm and her sweet fragrance. He wanted to take her in his arms and kiss her delectable mouth.

Those enchanting green eyes looked at him inquiringly. "Did your business go well this evening, sir?"

At the mention of where he'd been, Kit was filled with dread at the prospect of pursuing the unknown Lady Frey. He knew a sudden urge to confide in Victoria about what he was about to embark upon, then he realized he'd already asked her to keep far too many secrets from his mother and sister. How could he lay a heavier burden on her delicate shoulders? It would only cause her to worry about him if she knew that he might become a target of the very French spy he sought.

With a sigh, Kit knew he must explain his future absences without causing her pain. "Unfortunately, I find that government affairs shall keep me much occupied during our stay in London. I shall be unable to accompany you to the social events you ladies might wish to attend."

Victoria made a soft noise which Kit hoped was a disappointed sigh. "Do not worry about us, my lord. Your affairs are far more important than our frivolous amusements. I am certain we shall be able to manage on our own. We do not lack for gentlemen friends who will gladly escort us in your absence."

That's what Kit was afraid of. Just then, streams of people began to fill the hallway as the intermission ended. He reluctantly led his wife back to Lord Morton's party. All the young admirers were forced to return to where they belonged, leaving Kit the opportunity to sit beside Victoria through the rest of the performance.

Kit announced to Lord Morton that he would return his family to Grosvenor Square, then led the ladies down to the waiting family carriage. Isabel chattered about what she'd seen all the way home. Kit noted that only Victoria responded to the girl's comments. His mother sat quiet and glowering in the corner of the carriage.

As they entered Cranford House, Luisa snapped, "That is quite enough about the opera, Isabel." The dowager looked grim as she spoke to her daughter. "You won't get the least bit of sleep if you continue on in that manner. Do not forget there is Lady Morton's party tomorrow evening. I think you and Victoria should retire or we shall have to send our regrets. I need to speak with your brother alone."

Kit looked longingly at Victoria as she politely said her goodnights then accompanied his sister up the stairs. Her green eyes had been full of inquiry as she gazed curiously at his mother. He'd wanted to press a kiss upon her soft lips, but his irate parent had placed a possessive hand upon his arm, keeping him at her side and he would have appeared unfeeling of her distress to have pulled free from her to go to his wife.

After the ladies departed, he led his mother into the library and got her comfortably seated, offering to send for tea, but she declined. He poured himself a brandy, then settled opposite her. "What is this matter that is so urgent that it couldn't wait, *Mamãe*?"

The lady looked close to tears. "You saw for yourself what a success your wife was this evening, not that I blame her for she is lovely. But 'tis your sister we are trying to launch on the sea of matrimony. The child has had her head in those novels so long, she is expecting a handsome hero to magically step from the crowd and carry her to the altar. She was so agog at the sights that she took no notice that the gentleman scarcely were aware of her existence, not that a single one of them was tall enough to suit. It was just as I feared. My daughter is going to be a dismal failure and die an old maid. I do not think I can bear the humiliation.''

Quite used to his mother's complaining, Kit was struck more with the first part of her statement than the last. He'd hated seeing all those men crowded around ogling his desirable wife. His mother was correct, Victoria was a success. No matter where she went, she would have admirers crowding around her. How could he abandon her to the wiles of the practiced rakes who searched Society for any woman who took their fancy while he lured Lady Frey into a liaison? Victoria was an innocent in the ways of the Polite World.

Kit saw his mother was waiting for him to respond about her worries in regards to Isabel. ''Is it not far too early to be making such dire predictions about my sister? I think Isabel looked lovely tonight. I am certain her dance card will be filled tomorrow evening.'' As would Victoria's, he feared.

Lady Ridgecrest leaned over and grabbed his arm. ''Kit, you must go with us to Lady Morton's. I'll not have Isabel sitting out every dance.''

"Mamãe, I cannot dance with my sister or we should appear to be quite provincial. It would only spoil Isabel's chances to cut a dash.''

''But you can make other gentleman dance with her.''

Kit suddenly had this foolish vision of himself lurking round the edges of a dance floor with a dueling piston saying, *''Dance with Miss Harden or die.''*

He laughed, which caused his mother to frown. Sobering, he leaned forward and took her hand to calm her nerves. "My dear, I think you are being overly dramatic. It's far too early to determine my sister's success on the Marriage Mart. Besides, I cannot force gentlemen to dance with Isabel."

Lady Ridgecrest yanked her hand free, glaring at him with reproachful eyes. "I see it is going to be just as it was at Harwick. You have no feelings for what I suffer. Your family is to be abandoned to fend for ourselves while you go about your so important business."

Before Kit could respond, his mother rose and left the room in a huff, leaving him filled with remorse. She was right, he was about to engage in his clandestine business of unmasking a spy and the guilt over leaving his family unprotected was nearly overwhelming. Circumstances weren't as they'd been before. At Harwick, he'd been certain there was little that could happen to harm them. But they were in London now, with all its inherent pitfalls. Worse, what if the French agent already knew who he was, would his family be in danger? He needed a gentleman he could safely rely on who would accompany the ladies to their entertainments. But who the devil could he turn to? It would have to be someone he could trust completely.

Kit picked up his glass of brandy and was about to drink when his meeting with Major Cooper came to mind. The gentleman had given him his answer when he'd mentioned seeing Kit's cousin, Paul Harden. He was only a distant cousin, but he and Kit had formed a firm bond at Oxford. They'd exchanged brief letters over the years, but slowly they'd each become involved with their own affairs and drifted apart.

Would Paul come to help? The last he'd heard his

cousin was still unmarried, raising his invalid brother at his small estate in Essex. Paul would likely welcome a brief respite from his normal duties and responsibilities.

Kit realized he could ride to Chelmsford and back by tomorrow night. He would have to take his cousin completely into his confidence, but he'd trust Paul with his life. More importantly, Kit would be trusting Paul with the lives of the people most important to him.

CHAPTER EIGHT

Despite the late night, Victoria rose early the following morning, hoping for a little private conversation with her husband. She'd been disappointed when her mother-in-law had delayed him from coming upstairs. She was curious about what Luisa had discussed with her son, but no doubt she would find out today.

Upon arriving in the front hall, she discovered Kit dressed in a grey driving coat and donning a pair of York gloves.

Fear gripped her heart. Was he leaving them to again embark on some dangerous mission to Spain? There must have been something of her emotions evident on her face for he came to her, a gentle smile tipping his sculpted mouth.

"I am not abandoning you to my mother and sister again, my dear. Just a short journey into the country to visit an old family relation."

"Family? I did not know you had any relations who . . . that is . . ." Victoria faltered to a finish, not knowing how to describe his family's dispute. She'd heard only bits and pieces of the story about the Duke of Townsend's disowning his son years earlier due to his marriage to a Portuguese wine merchant's daughter. She was under the impression that there had been little communication between Kit and his father's family.

Kit laughed wryly. "Oh, we have Harden relatives in England, but most have never acknowledged our existence nor we theirs. But that is old family history. I have a long journey and I must ask a favor."

"Of course."

"Promise you will not leave for Lady Morton's Ball without me. I should very much like to accompany you." His dark gaze intently watched her.

Victoria felt a rush of pleasure that he wanted to come with her. "I . . . er we shall be pleased to await you, sir."

Kit titled her chin up and pressed a soft kiss on her lips. He lingered longer than was proper, then seemed to remember himself. "Until this evening, my dear."

With a swirl of his cape, he disappeared out the front door, leaving his wife with a sense of wistful yearning that she might spend the day with him. The sound of a door closing behind her brought her from her musing and she turned to see Matthews.

"Good morning, my lady. Shall I inform Cook you are ready to be served breakfast?"

With a sigh, Victoria said yes, then strolled past the butler as he held the breakfast parlour door for her.

Victoria ate her meal, filled with a feeling of supreme happiness that her relationship with her husband was growing. Kit wished to accompany her to the ball tonight. She had visions of twirling about the floor in a waltz with him. At last they would get the opportunity to spend time together.

She'd spent two long months waiting to again see the man she'd married. Now he'd returned from the Peninsula unharmed and she no longer needed to fear for his safety. Hopefully they would be able to enjoy their visit to London, not just getting to know one another, but to develop a genuine affection. Then they would return to Harwick, to begin their lives as man and wife. Victoria's cheeks warmed as she thought of Kit sharing her bed, but her heart beat faster at the possibility.

The door to the breakfast parlour opened and Matthews entered, a frown on his round face. "My lady, the housekeeper has requested you come upstairs at your earliest convenience."

Victoria's dreams were abruptly interrupted. The young bride's fantasies were lost amid the mundane duties of the mistress of the house. Thoughts of the coming ball were soon put aside as Victoria found that life in a family was always complicated. She had to deal with her mother-in-law's attempt to dismiss an upstairs maid. Victoria was beginning to think that much of her life would be spent engaging new servants to replace the ones the capricious lady turned off with such regularity.

After some fifteen minutes, Victoria at last convinced Luisa that the household servants were in truth employed by the Marquess of Cranford whose town house they leased while that gentleman was in the Indies. Therefore the servants couldn't be discharged. The lady complained bitterly, saying that no one cared about her wishes—not her daughter, who was wearing the pale rose dress instead of the white Luisa chose, not her son, who was ignoring her wishes to accompany them to the ball, nor her new daughter-in-law, who was forcing her to tolerate an incompetent maid.

Victoria assured the lady that Isabel appeared lovely in the rose gown, Kit was to escort them that evening and she would send her own maid, Betty, to Luisa if that was what the lady wished. Within a short time, the dowager was full of apology for her upset, attributing it to nerves about their first London entertainment.

The day seemed to fly by, and before Victoria knew it they were dressing for the party. The maid had just finished doing up the tiny buttons on her evening gown when Victoria heard sounds coming from the adjoining bedchamber. Her heart raced at the thought she would see her husband in a few minutes.

About to descend to the drawing room, she was summoned to first Isabel's room to oversee the finishing touches, then to the dowager's room to help with final decisions about what looked best on the former beauty. Victoria was amazed to find that quite as much time was devoted to getting the dowager dressed as Isabel, for as her mother-in-law informed her, who knew what dreadful things the old duke had been saying about her for years.

At last the ladies were satisfied with their appearance and went down to join Lord Ridgecrest in the drawing room. Victoria thought Kit was excessively handsome in a simple black evening coat with white waistcoat and white knee breeches. His hair was neatly brushed into a Brutus style, which suited his dark looks.

"Good evening, ladies." Kit bowed then took his turn admiring the ladies. Luisa wore a dark blue satin gown trimmed with black lace that matched her man-

tilla. Isabel had on a round robe of rose net-crape
worn over a white silk under-dress. Her dark curls
were adorned with small clusters of miniature roses.

At last he came to Victoria. He praised her gown
of green cobweb muslin over white satin with gold
ribband and sash, as well as her red curls topped with
a simple gold cornet fashioned like tiny gold leaves.
An amorous glitter came to his dark eyes. For just a
moment their gazes locked and Victoria felt breathless, then Isabel interrupted.

"We shall be late, Kit."

The viscount reluctantly drew his gaze from his
beautiful wife. "We shan't be late, Isabel. Besides,
there is something important I wish to tell you before
we depart."

The ladies took their seats and looked at him expectantly. Kit was certain that at least one of them wasn't
going to like what he was about to say. "I spoke with
our cousin, Paul Harden, today. He is coming to
Town on business so I invited him to stay with us."

Kit thought it best not to tell the ladies Paul's true
reason for coming. His cousin had been surprised,
but delighted to see Kit. Once the reason was
revealed, it had taken little to convince the gentleman
to come and help keep Kit's family safe. In truth
Paul's young brother Norman, hearing only of the
proposed visit to Town, had been delighted about
the prospect of coming to London, that is if he might
come as well, for he longed to visit the metropolis.
And so it had been decided that both brothers would
stay in Grosvenor Square.

The dowager was on her feet in an instant, her
voice taut with anger. "You have invited one of the
Duke of Townsend's nephews to stay here? His Grace
insulted me in the most outrageous manner thirty

years ago. Not one of his relations has ever sought us out to welcome us to England and now you invite this man to our home.''

"*Mamãe*, Paul and I were friends at Oxford. He is acquainted with the duke, but hardly close. As to why he has never visited Harwick, he is raising a younger brother who is crippled and rarely travels, but I was certain you wouldn't hold that against the lad who wishes to come to London to see the sights.''

Lady Ridgecrest stalked across the room to stand before the fireplace. "Whatever will we do with a young boy underfoot? They are so noisy, and messy and always requiring feeding.''

"Norman is fifteen and a scholar and Isabel's chattering is more likely to bother him.'' Kit sighed. He'd known his mother would balk at having any of his father's family come, but he was desperate. There was no other person to whom he could entrust the safety of the ladies. '' 'Twas you who pointed out last night that I would be engaged with my own affairs here in Town. I thought you might enjoy having Paul to escort you about in the evenings.''

Victoria who'd been startled by the vehemence of her mother-in-law's outburst, rose and went to the lady. Hoping to convince Luisa that none of the responsibility would fall on her shoulders, Victoria said, "I should be delighted to have Mr. Harden and his brother join us. I am certain the young man will be pleased to do all the things which Isabel has suggested we do since we came to Town, like visit the Tower, or Astley's Circus, if he is able.''

Isabel, who'd been sitting quietly, rose and came to her mother's side. She too had long felt slighted by the rest of the Harden family, but the possibility of visiting the Circus curbed her rancor at the old hurt. "I suppose it would be pleasant to meet some of our English relations at last, *Mamãe*. After all, it has been nearly thirty years since Papa and the duke quarreled."

Kit decided to use his trump card. "Isabel is correct. Let us forget old hurts. Besides, Paul's mother was an old school friend to Sally Jersey. He's promised to do what he can to procure vouchers for Almack's for you ladies."

The dowager might be Portuguese and have lived the last four years isolated in the country, but even she had heard of Almack's and knew the significance of what the coveted vouchers would mean for her daughter. "Well, far be it from me to keep the little crippled lad from coming to Town. I should be happy to meet these Hardens as long as they have nothing against us."

Just then Matthew entered and announced that the carriage was at the door. Victoria, intent on appeasing Luisa about the proposed visit of Mr. Paul Harden, suddenly realized this might be the last night Kit would accompany them. He'd warned her he would be busy and she would not see much of him over the remainder of the Season. Well, she had tonight at least. She determined she would be happy and enjoy the evening with him.

Lady Morton's small party was in fact a crush of over a hundred guests invited to squeeze into Moore House in Berkeley Square. Victoria soon realized the error of her thinking that she might find time to be with her husband. The hostess, upon seeing Lord Ridgecrest, soon took him away to introduce to friends. Before the lady did so, however, she intro-

duced Victoria, Isabel and Luisa to a group of young
ladies and matrons who stood waiting for the music to
begin. The dowager, not wishing to dance, wandered
away with several ladies of similar age to discuss the
trials and tribulations of launching a young lady into
Society.

Victoria and Isabel were soon surrounded by a
group of gentlemen, each hoping to find a young
lady with whom they could stand up. Unfortunately,
Isabel towered over most of men, but to Victoria's
delight one gentleman seemed quite enchanted with
the large lady.

When the first strains of the music filled the ballroom, Victoria looked hopefully for her husband, but
he was in conversation with several military gentlemen on the opposite side of the dance floor. He
seemed not to notice that the music had begun, so
intent was his conversation. Covering her disappointment, she accepted the offer of a dashing young man
who'd been introduced as Lord Rowe.

Across the ballroom, Kit was listening to the details
of the battle of Sabugal where the allies had routed
the French from several army officers recently
returned from Portugal. Looking up, he was suddenly
aware that the dancing had begun. He caught sight
of Victoria, her cheeks flushed from the exercise. He
was surprised at the wave of jealousy which rushed
through him as he saw the gentleman who led her
down the line of dancers. How absurd it was to resent
a man who was simply dancing with his wife, he
thought, then shifted his gaze to his sister.

Isabel promenaded past him, clearly enjoying herself with an unknown gentleman. Kit closely surveyed
her partner. The man was handsome and cultured.
His clothes were of the first stare of fashion, but

one wouldn't call him a dandy, for his collar points weren't excessively high or his coat overly ornate or hued. Still there was that about him that suggested a great deal of attention to his appearance. Kit was very curious why a sophisticated man of Town would take notice of a dowerless, green girl like his sister. Kit loved Isabel but even he must own she was no diamond of the first water.

"Colonel Godwin, who is that fellow partnering the tall dark lady in the rose gown?"

The officer squinted a bit then said, "Oh, just one of those Frenchies you find underfoot at every fashionable do. Are you acquainted with the lady?"

" 'Tis my sister, sir."

"Ah, well the Marquis de Athier has been in England for years trying to rally enough of his countrymen to return and drive Bonaparte from the throne. Don't know his circumstances, but a good many of those fellows have more titles than money, so best warn Miss Harden to have a care."

Kit was far more worried that it was a Frenchman who danced with his sister, since he himself was seeking a French spy, than about the man's funds. Lord Carew had suggested they might seek Kit out if they learned he was part of his lordship's network. Was it possible they would try to get information from his sister? It was the very thing that he'd feared.

He would warn Paul to keep a close eye on this de Athier if the man pursued his acquaintance with Isabel. Hopefully, the Frenchman, if he were something other than what he appeared, would soon realize that his sister knew nothing of Kit's activities.

From his left, Kit heard a familiar voice. "Well if it isn't Kit Harden. I'm delighted to see you've finally escaped your responsibilities in the country and come

to Town. Why I've not seen you since we hired that
fellow to release a crate of doves in the don's house
in Oxford six years ago."

Kit turned to see Jack Freeman, a former school
comrade, now wearing regimentals, coming towards
him, with a stunning blond beauty in a blue striped
silk gown on his arm. Kit was flooded with memories
of those carefree years at school when the only thing
he'd had to worry about was being sent down for a
foolish prank.

"Jack, 'tis good to see you. But what is this? Never
knew you were mad for the army."

The captain shook his head and grinned. "Not I.
'Tis the disadvantage of being a younger son. My
father was mad to see me out from under foot and
with a profession. So here I am, marching and taking
orders, but 'tis not a bad life. The ladies love the red
jackets. Ain't that so, my dear? But allow me to present
you to my lovely companion who requested an introduction to you. Eve, this is Christopher Harden, Viscount Ridgecrest. Kit, may I present Lady Frey."

Kit never betrayed the shock which raced through
him at the lady's name. In some way Lady Frey had
ferreted out the information that he worked for Lord
Carew and had come for what? Information about
the others who were gathering intelligence or for Kit's
very life? Was this the woman who was responsible for
the death of four brave men?

He raised his hand, which he would have preferred
to put around her perfidious white throat, but instead
grasped the gloved hand she extended to him and
reluctantly lifted it to his lips. "My lady, always a
pleasure to meet a beautiful woman."

"My lord, I am delighted to encounter a handsome
new member to Society. I do not believe I have ever

seen you in Town before." The lady fluttered her
long lashes in a practiced manner.

"Haven't been to London since my salad days with
Jack here. Inherited a ramshackle estate which has
kept me busy. But this year duty called."

Lady Frey seemed more alert. "Duty, my lord?"

"That's what my mother calls the matter. Had to
properly launch my sister in Society."

Kit was certain he detected a look of disappointment in the lady's face but it was gone so quickly only
someone observing her closely would have seen it.
Just then the music came to an end and the dancers
cleared the floor.

"Jack, I'm going to claim the privilege of an old
friend and steal your companion for the next dance.
If you are free, Lady Frey?"

"I should be delighted, my lord."

Kit led the lady onto the floor where the strains of
a waltz were beginning. He resisted the urge to look
for Victoria. He was supposed to be embarking on a
flirtation with the woman before him, not wearing
his heart on his sleeve for his wife.

"So, Lord Ridgecrest, how does a country gentleman amuse himself when he comes to London?"

"Why, any way he can, my dear lady." Kit's voice
was full of innuendo.

She looked up at him coyly through her lashes.
"My lord, I think you can be quite wicked."

"When given the opportunity, my lady."

The lady's laughter rang out, causing heads to turn.

Victoria, who'd been reminding Isabel that she
could not yet waltz in public, turned to see her husband take a dashing blond woman into his arms and
twirl the lady round the floor. A mixture of anger
and hurt warred in her breast. He'd not seen fit to

ask his own wife for a dance, yet there he was holding some female who was simpering and laughing at him. Did he have so little interest in getting to know the woman he'd married, Victoria wondered? Or did he merely prefer a different type of woman than the one circumstances had forced upon him?

With a heavy heart Victoria turned to Lord Morton, who came to ask her for a dance and to later go down to supper with him. She forced a bright smile to her face, but suddenly there was no longer any joy in the ball for her.

The carriage drew to a halt barely one block from Lady Morton's town house on an empty dark street. A gentleman stepped from the shadows of a doorway and into the vehicle whose curtains had been drawn. The coachman looked around, but seeing no one about in the dim gaslight's glow, he set the horses into a slow gait homeward.

René could tell by the look on Eve's face that something was wrong. "Our prey was not interested in the bait?"

"Don't be ridiculous," Eve snapped. "The problem is not Ridgecrest. The man has asked to drive out with me tomorrow. I shall have him in my bed by the end of the week if that is what I wish. I have been wanting to speak to you all night. My footman came home earlier this evening and told me there has been a man asking questions about me in the neighborhood taverns."

"Haven't gone back to your former profession to earn a bit extra, now have you?" René grinned maliciously.

Eve gave him a disdainful look. "Will you think this

so amusing when you are having your neck stretched at the end of an English rope, René?''

The Frenchman leaned back against the squabs. This new intelligence of a stranger asking questions couldn't be ignored. "And your servant was positive this is no slighted lover or . . . former patron from your days on the street?"

The lady angrily shook her head. "Peter described him and I am certain I know no such man. René, we must give up this deep game we play or we shall be caught. We have all but finished Lord Carew's operation. Let us leave for Paris tonight."

"Not yet. I want to know if Ridgecrest has any useful information. For all we know they have recruited new men to replace those we eliminated."

Eve folded her arms stubbornly and shook her head. "I'll not risk my life any longer on false promises of going to Paris. 'Tis easy for you to say we must stay, but you don't have someone asking people all manner of questions regarding *you*."

René crossed the coach aisle and slid onto the seat beside Eve. He took her into his arms and trailed soft kisses along the line of her throat as she tried to resist his advances. "Just this last one, *ma petite*. Stay one more week. Don't do anything to draw the attention of this man who you think trails you. Act as if Ridgecrest is merely a new lover. If the viscount gives you no information, then I shall take matters into my hands."

Eve stared at René realizing he meant the handsome young viscount she'd danced with that evening would be found dead on some country road. It caused her not the least pang. "Once you finish with this English spy we leave for France?"

"I promise that by this time next week we shall be boarding my yacht for France."

Eve sighed, surrendering to her lover's sweet embrace. "Then I shall do my best."

As the Harden family carriage rolled toward Cranford House, Kit only half listened as his mother exclaimed excitedly over winning some twenty pounds playing whist. The dowager had made friends and was full of excitement about her first taste of Society. Isabel and Victoria sat quietly in their corners contributing little to the conversation, but in actuality it was more a running monologue on Luisa's part.

Kit's mind was too full of the implications of his encounter with Lady Frey to pay much heed. He knew he must speak with Lord Carew tonight to inform him that the lady had some means of finding out who worked for his lordship.

When the carriage drew up at last, Kit followed the ladies into the foyer then announced he had another engagement. As he bade them good night, he noted that Victoria turned away coolly and went up the stairs with only the briefest of nods.

She was angry with him for ignoring her so completely that evening and he couldn't blame her. A part of him wanted to go after her and explain why he'd kept his distance at Lady Morton's, but he thought it best she remain incensed. A hostile wife was the perfect excuse for his appearing to seek comfort elsewhere. He would have to be discreet to keep the rumors from reaching her. He was certain he could bring her around once they captured this spy and he was able to reveal the truth.

Reluctantly, Kit returned to the carriage and

ordered the coachman to take him to Park Lane. Within minutes, the vehicle drew to a halt in front of Carew House where lights still blazed.

An ancient butler led Kit into his lordship's library where the earl was seated at his desk, a half-full glass of brandy at his elbow as he worked over some documents.

The old man was still fully dressed, but his neck-cloth had been loosened. Spying the viscount, Lord Carew sat back. "Christopher, is something amiss?"

"Lady Frey made herself known to me this evening. It would seem your suspicious about her were correct."

" 'Tis the Runner's suspicion. He brought me news tonight as well. He thinks he found two ruffians who work for her but doing what we don't know." The earl handed Kit a piece of paper. "Visit these lads and find out why they paid the lady a visit two nights ago and we might find out what she's up to."

Kit looked at the names and direction of the two men. St. Giles's was one of the worst slums of London. If he valued his life, Kit knew it was a place he should only visit during the light of day.

"I'll go first thing in the morning." Kit was to take Lady Frey driving in the afternoon. It might help if he knew some of her secrets before their meeting.

"I'll have Grafton meet you at your town house at eight o'clock in the morning."

Kit nodded. The sooner he ended this unsavory business the sooner he could set things to right with Victoria and that was something he longed to do.

CHAPTER NINE

The morning sun hovered behind the tops of the buildings as Kit and Mr. Grafton drove into St. Giles's rookeries. On the advice of the Runner, Kit had brought along the largest of the grooms employed at Cranford House, due to the danger one might encounter in the blind alleys of London's most notorious slum.

Even that early in the morning, the streets were filled with the drunks, prostitutes and thieves who never seemed to disappear from sight in that part of Town. Several of the women called to the passing carriage of men attempting to earn a little even at that early hour, but Kit kept his team moving forward as he followed Mr. Grafton's directions.

Finally they arrived at a dark, filthy street corner which the Runner signaled as their destination. Kit was certain they were being observed from the surrounding buildings by suspicious eyes, but there were no signs of any living being in the dwellings. He set the large groom to watch the curricle, making certain a dueling pistol was noticeable through the front of the hulking groom's grey coat.

Mr. Grafton led the way down a littered alley which ended at a weathered door. Without a knock, the Runner entered the building and hurried up a flight of stairs. Kit followed, wondering about the wretched lives of the people who inhabited these crumbling structures. He made a solemn promise to himself that when he acquired the dukedom and a seat in the House of Lords, he'd try to improve conditions for the poor souls in London. But that was for later, now he must concentrate on the matter at hand.

At last they were positioned in front of a door which seemed to hang on one hinge. The Runner withdrew a small pistol and nodded to Kit. They burst into the small room. At least ten people, ranging in ages from young to old, were on the floor asleep.

"What ta bloody 'ell?" An ancient man with stained yellow teeth sat up and rubbed his eyes. Seeing the armed men, he yelled, "Run lads, 'tis ta Red Breasts."

Grafton stood blocking the door. "I'll let daylight into any one of you what moves."

By now the entire room of ruffians were sitting up staring at the pair who'd invaded their sanctuary. Even in the dim light pouring through the grimy window, Kit was certain he'd never seen a filthier lot of men and boys. "We mean you no harm. We've only come to ask a few questions."

A short red-haired lad scratched his head and yawned as he eyed the men. Sensing no immediate danger, he said, "Would ye look at this 'ere, lads. Ta nobs are comin' to the rookeries ta learn what's what. Well, what ye want to know gov'ner?"

"I should like to speak with one Dickey West or

his friend, Jimmy the Hands.'' Those were the names of the two that Grafton had trailed back to St. Giles's two nights hence.

A lad in the back instantly stated, "Never 'eard of 'em.''

"Now, Dick, don't be tryin' to cozen us." Mr. Grafton smiled as he recognized the lad.

The young thief looked as if he were about to jump out the second-story window, which Kit suspected he might be able to do if he were a housebreaker. But the portal looked as if it hadn't been opened in years.

"How would you like to earn some easy rhino, Dick?''

" 'Ow easy and 'ow much?''

"Come into the hall. I would say the more you can tell me, the larger the reward.''

He was doubtful, but willing to hear the gentry cove out since blunt might be gained. Dickey threw off his tattered blanket and followed the gent into the hall. He never gave Jimmy, who was huddled by the window with his blanket covering his face, a glance.

Even if Dickey didn't know what the man wanted he realized he might be able to chouse a few coins from him. What he didn't like was the Red Breast standin' there pointin' that barkin' iron, especially since Dickey knew he still had a few bits of Lady Frey's silver still hidden under the loose board near his makeshift bed.

The gentleman and the housebreaker stood facing one another in the hall as the runner kept his eye on the assorted footpads, thieves and files who strained to hear what Dickey would say. It was an unwritten law of the rookeries that one didn't squeak beef on his mates and they wanted to make certain the lad followed the rules.

"Dick, Mr. Grafton here tells me you visited with Lady Frey in Half Moon Street two nights ago. Went right to the front door like an invited guest."

Dickey was beginning to sweat now. He'd told Jimmy the lady would never come lookin' for her property, since what she was doin' was very 'avy-cavy, but maybe he was wrong. With an air of false bravado, he grinned at the gent. "So, a handsome gent like me knows lots of morts."

Kit crossed his arms and looked down at the lad. "Don't take me for a flat if you want your money. Why did you visit the lady?"

Dickey cut his eyes back to the Runner, who was glarin' at him somethin' fierce. What did he owe that hoity-toity wench with all her airs? She'd put a blade to his throat and ordered him not to return and only gave him half his usual fee. Here was a chance to get her back. " 'Twere nothin' bad. Ta lady 'ired me to follow a nob down on Parliament Street."

Kit straightened. "Who, Dick?"

"Flash cull name of C'roo, Lord C'roo."

Despite the lad's St. Giles Greek, Kit recognized Lord Carew's name. "And what did the lady want from the lord?"

"Wanted ta names of 'is mates. Them what left with 'im at night."

Had it truly been that simple to nearly put an end to the network? Had the earl's habit of always taking his men to drink at his club been the weak link to their secrecy? "How many names did you give the lady?"

"Five, maybe six o'er the last few years. The old gent usually rode off alone so the money weren't all that good."

The source of the names was now exposed, but

there was one more thing Kit wanted to know. "Was the lady alone when you met with her?"

Dickey shook his head. "Was usually a gentry cove like yerself with ta lady, but 'e took care I ne'er seen 'is face. Tall, 'e were with black hair."

So, Lady Frey had an accomplice. Kit wasn't surprised. He dug a coin from his pocket. "You have earned your money, Dick, but be warned the lady was involved in a hanging offense. Don't go near Lord Carew again."

The thief's eyes grew round and he nodded vigorously. But when the gentleman placed the coin in his hand his face relaxed into a smile. "A yellow boy!"

Kit signaled to Mr. Grafton and they hurried down the stairs.

Dickey bit the coin and to his delight found it real. "Ye can come anytime, Runner, long as ye bring the gov'ner."

The two men hurried back to the carriage. As Kit tooled back to Grosvenor Square he knew they were closer to finding the French spies. All they needed was the name of Lady Frey's accomplice and his job would be done. He would at last be able to return to his family, but most especially to his wife. The last prospect caused him to flick his reins to gain a bit of speed from his cattle.

Cranford House was a buzz of activities that day preparing for the arrival of Mr. Harden and his brother. Victoria had risen determined to put her disappointment about Kit's disinterest in her aside and she knew no better way than to immerse herself in work. She consulted Cook about the menu, inspected the bedchambers to make certain they were properly aired and personally arranged flowers for each of the visitors' rooms.

She'd seen nothing of her husband and forced herself not to inquire of his whereabouts. If he wanted to speak with her he could find *her*.

Luisa had accepted an invitation for tea with her new friend, Lady Forrester, but Isabel had steadfastly refused to accompany her mother, saying that Victoria needed her assistance. While the viscountess was touched by her sister-in-law's gracious gesture, she found Isabel to be more often in the way than helpful. At last she sent the young miss to the Green Drawing Room to sort the deluge of invitations which had arrived following their introduction to Society. She gave Isabel the responsibility of deciding which they should accept and which to send their regrets, for it mattered little to Victoria since Kit would not be accompanying them.

Finally finished with her tasks, Victoria joined Isabel and they began to discuss whether it should be Lady Marringham's Rout or the Countess of Hairston's musicale for the following evening. The drawing room door opened and Victoria looked up hoping that at last Kit had come to join them.

She was disappointed to see Matthews who announced, "Mr. Paul Harden, Mr. Norman Harden, my lady."

Victoria rose, then halted in amazement. A man and a boy entered the chamber, but man did not correctly describe the gentleman, he was a veritable colossus. He appeared well over six foot, with shoulders so broad they almost brushed the door facings as he stepped through the portal. Barrel-chested, he stood on great sturdy limbs which gave him more the look of a country farmer than a gentleman. His tanned face, which one would describe as interesting, instead of handsome, with an aquiline nose and high cheekbones, was framed by blond hair trimmed neatly around his visage. Mr. Harden's attire was clearly the work of some provincial tailor, for there was nothing about him, from his simply tied cravat to his plain grey waistcoat under a loosely fitted olive green coat, that was fashionable.

By contrast his young brother came barely to Mr. Harden's shoulder. Norman was slender without being frail. He was a handsome lad, his blond hair a shade darker than his brother's but his eyes were the same pale blue as his sibling's. He was dressed in a dark blue superfine coat with grey and white striped waistcoat, but the cut was no better than his brother's. The only hint that the boy was crippled was a slight limp as he stepped towards the ladies.

Victoria greeted their visitors, introducing herself and Isabel. Miss Harden had suddenly become quiet, surveying these heretofore unknown relations who had so thoroughly ignored much of Kit's family.

Tea was ordered and the group settled down to become better acquainted. It soon became apparent to Victoria that Norman Harden had no interest in such plebeian entertainment as Astley's Circus or the Tower. The young man had a great interest in science which included steam engines and the new pneumatic lifts which were said to be in use at the London foundries. After Norman went on for some time about Mr. Trevithick's steam locomotive, Paul suggested to his brother that he not bore the ladies with such nonsense.

Victoria smiled kindly at the boy, liking his enthusiasm even though not understanding much of what he spoke of. Then she inquired how long Mr. Harden's business would keep him in Town.

Paul's brows rose. Unaware that the ladies were in the dark as to his reason for being there, he replied, "Why, as long as Kit has need of me."

Victoria looked up from the cup of tea she was pouring. "Need? I understood that you came to London to transact some business, sir."

Paul grinned at his hostess. "My business is to make certain you ladies are properly looked after and escorted to your entertainments."

Isabel, who'd been looking over the cakes for the one that took her fancy, selected a small cream bun. "What you mean is my brother asked you to come so he wouldn't be bothered with us."

"Now, Miss Harden, that is not the case at all. Kit thought—"

Indignation evident on her face, Victoria set her cup of tea down. "My husband thought that we needed a keeper. Is that not true?"

Before Mr. Harden could explain Kit's motives, Matthews arrived to announce a caller. Victoria struggled to suppress her anger at Kit's lack of faith in her. Mr. Harden's presence was evidence that he didn't trust her to manage things. Regaining her composure, she instructed the butler to show the visitor in.

The Marquis de Athier strolled into the drawing room. The Frenchman far outshone the Harden brothers in his style of dress. He was elegant in a dove grey morning coat and pale yellow waistcoat. His Hessians gleamed in the morning light. He came forward and gallantly kissed the ladies' hands, lingering a bit longer than was proper over Isabel's.

Introductions were made, then the Frenchman settled down to inform them of the latest *on-dits* he'd gleaned that very morning. But Victoria scarcely listened. Her mind still dwelled on Kit having brought his cousin to London to watch over them, like they were errant children who needed a guardian. It was very clear he still hadn't forgiven her for taking estate matters into her hands and for bringing the ladies to London, no matter his apology.

At that moment the marquis drew Victoria back into the conversation by inquiring if he might take Miss Harden driving in the Park the following day. Her sister-in-law expressed her desire to join the gentleman, but Victoria was certain Kit wouldn't approve of the unknown marquis, and there was something about the gentleman with his piercing stare which she did not like. Determined to prove to her husband she was responsible, she coolly informed the Frenchman, that at present their plans were uncertain and perhaps he might take Isabel at a later date.

The marquis stayed only the requisite time, then properly said his goodbyes. The door had barely closed behind him, when Paul Harden rose and stood in front of the fireplace. Hands on his hips, he addressed himself to Isabel. "I can see why Kit thought you needed someone to look out for you if you've been encouraging that dirty dish, cousin."

The young lady's dark eyes flashed fire. "How dare you impugn a titled gentleman like the marquis?"

Norman, who'd slumped boredly into his chair as he tried to balance a spoon on the edge of a nearby table, showed a spark of amusement when his brother remarked, "A French title, Miss Harden, is worthless with Bonaparte running France. Likely there are no estates left to provide any income."

Victoria, seeing the red warning flags rise on Isabel's cheeks, thought it was best to intercede. "Mr. Harden, the marquis is only a recent acquaintance. There is no serious attachment between he and dear Isabel."

Paul glanced at his outraged cousin. Perhaps he'd come on a bit strong for their first meeting. He knew Kit wouldn't want his sister cavorting with a Frenchman, considering what the viscount was at present undertaking. Paul decided to try a bit of charm on the ladies. "No doubt you are correct, Lady Victoria. I hope that you and Miss Harden will call me Cousin, for that is what I am, although once removed."

Isabel rose, her mouth a thin line of disapproval. "Well, Cousin, I think I can safely speak for Victoria when I say welcome to London but we'd prefer that your cousinly nose be *removed* from our affairs."

With that, the young lady sailed from the room.

Norman Harden chuckled. "A proper set down, if I ever heard one, dear brother."

"Mind your tongue, lad. I can and will box your ears."

"Lady Victoria, you see what a brute I have endured lo these many years." Norman grinned at his hostess, showing not the least fear of his brother. "Perchance you will show me my room before Paul decides we all need a proper thrashing to be kept in line."

Victoria was uncertain what to make of Mr. Paul Harden. She led young Norman to his bedchamber, leaving his brother staring out the rear window into the garden, a thoughtful expression on his face. Just before Norman closed the door to his room he stopped his hostess. "You know my brother is generally not so rag-mannered. He's a bit managing but I think it comes from having run our family estate since he was so young. Seems to think everyone should fall in with his orders."

She smiled reassuringly at the young man, for he was no part of her husband's plot. "Oh, I'm certain your brother was only following my husband's instruction to protect us from our own folly."

That fact still rankled Victoria a great deal. She had gone from longing to see Kit that very morning to determination to avoid the man who trusted her so little. Her spirits decidedly low, she made her way back to the drawing room where she still must face the unpleasant task of introducing her mother-in-law to their guests upon the volatile lady's return.

Avoiding Lord Ridgecrest turned out to be surprisingly easy for Victoria over the next several days. He was rarely to be found at home in Grosvenor Square and their paths rarely crossed at the entertainments the ladies and Mr. Harden chose to attend.

To Victoria's surprise, Luisa had been completely charmed by their giant of a cousin. It had only taken a few compliments to the aging widow and his whispered assurances that he'd always thought the duke a complete dotard. He promised the lady that with Kit so often gone, she might rely upon him to keep Miss Harden from forming any unsuitable alliances. Soon the dowager was proclaiming him a true gentleman.

Matters between Isabel and Paul, however, did not improve. Hostilities were renewed the following morning at breakfast as Isabel thumbed through the new invitations that had arrived.

"Oh, Victoria, there is to be a masked ball given by the Countess of Beckingham in two weeks. Can we not go? I have always envisioned myself as Diana the Huntress at such an affair.''

Before Victoria could comment, Paul looked up from the heaping plate of sliced ham and buttered eggs on which he'd been making considerable inroads. "Masked ball! Only the veriest hoyden would attend such a common affair. Believe me, my girl, you can have no notion of how very vulgar such affairs can be when people can hide their identities behind costumes.''

Isabel crushed a piece of toast between her fingers even as she gave her cousin an angry smile. "If they are such vulgar affairs, how come you have attended them?''

"Never set foot in one, nor had the least desire to do so. But one hears such shocking tales.''

Miss Harden's eyes had a dangerous glitter. "Never had the least desire to attend one? More likely you were certain that were you to don a domino you would still be recognized for the odious oak that you are.''

Paul glared across the table at his cousin. "You, my dear cousin, are a spoiled brat.''

"And you, sir, are a prosing provincial!''

Victoria set her teacup down so suddenly, that she hit her spoon which shot off to the floor. As Paul bent to retrieve the utensil, she calmly said, "That will be quite enough bickering from the pair of you. I would like you both to apologize and remember that we shall be staying together over the course of the next few weeks. Try to remember that you are a gentleman and you a lady.''

The twosome looked rather belligerently at one another, then offered half-hearted apologies.

Certain that was likely the best she could expect at the moment, Victoria rose. "Come Isabel, we are promised to join Lady Morton shopping this morning.''

Things did not improve over the next few days. While the pair rarely argued, they continued to hurl veiled barbs at one another. Only occasionally did matters come to a full-blown argument, but upon seeing Victoria, the couple would then attempt to return to frosty civility. It was quite amazing, for individually each was quite charming and pleasant, but when thrown together, they were like a pair of prize-fighters determined to land the winning verbal blow.

Luisa merely chuckled about her daughter's quarrels with her cousin, but then she was rarely there to witness them, being much involved with her new-found friends, Lady Forrester and Mrs. Whatley. With Norman being locked in the library with his studies, or off inspecting some new scientific marvel, Victoria was very often the sole observer of the couple's spats. She began to feel like a diplomatic intermediary between warring countries.

Each day soon seemed much like the day before to Victoria. There were rounds of Venetian breakfasts, musicales, balls and routs. Very shortly she was longing for the peace and tranquility of the country, finding little joy in her busy life in Town. There were always the same people to be met, some new scandal to be discussed and then they returned to their homes to begin anew the next day.

But Victoria had run her father's estate. She missed the feeling of doing something useful. She longed to return to Harwick where there were things needing to be done. Or was it that she knew she'd have more of an opportunity to see her husband at the remote estate?

After her first rush of anger at his high-handedness

in bringing Paul to Town, she'd calmed down and realized he had only meant it for the best. But as the days passed and he made no attempt to join her, she was filled with a wistfulness about the dreams and plans which she'd made during the two months she awaited his return. What had been especially disconcerting for Victoria was learning from her sister-in-law that Kit had taken the time to seek out Isabel and warn her away from de Athier, calling him a penniless rogue. It was clear he had far more interest in his sister's affairs than in his unwanted wife's.

One morning near the end of the week Victoria surprisingly found herself with no family problems to occupy her. Isabel had announced she would stay in her room and rest, declaring herself burnt to the socket, then Luisa left to attend some afternoon card party with Lady Forrester. With no one to oversee, the vigilant Paul decided to accompany his brother to Soho to visit a foundry which had recently installed a pneumatic lift.

In the hope of raising her flagging spirits, Victoria decided to visit Hatchard's. Perhaps a good book might at least distract her from her melancholy. She ordered the carriage. Leaving Betty on the bench outside the bookseller's, she entered the store in Piccadilly and soon was lost among the rows of literature. She'd selected several volumes for herself, then knowing Isabel's love of novels, Victoria decided to choose a few for her sister-in-law.

She'd just pulled one of Mary Meake's books from the shelf when a familiar voice came from behind the stacks.

Lady Morton's loud voice carried over the noise of the other customers. " 'I cannot believe that Lord Ridgecrest could be so unfeeling to dear Lady Victoria. Are you certain it was his lordship you saw with Lady Frey at Richmond Hill? I had heard the lady was involved with the Comte d'Caille.''

A voice Victoria didn't recognize chuckled, then said, ''Of course, I'm sure. d'Caille is old news. There is little doubt it was Ridgecrest with the widow. I suspect he is having an affair with the lady. No doubt, they are trying to be discreet, but despite the out-of-the-way places they visit, someone often reports seeing them. Disgraceful is what it is with him being newly married. I hear the poor *comte*'s heart is broken.''

Lady Morton sniffed. ''Heart, humbug. I think that organ had little to do with that affair.''

Victoria's own heart felt as if it had been pierced by a sharp instrument. It was far worse than she'd ever imagined. Her husband was not merely disinterested in her, but actually involved with another woman. The beautiful Lady Frey.

The image of the laughing blond beauty from Lady Morton's ball rose in Victoria's mind. A shudder of humiliation surged through her as the pair behind the books continued to discuss Victoria's husband and mistress.

All she could think of was that she must get out of there at once. She pushed the books haphazardly back on the stacks and hurried from the store. Her thoughts were so disordered that she walked blindly past Betty and would have continued on if the maid hadn't leapt to her feet and called her mistress's name.

''My lady, are you ill?''

''Ill?'' Rational thought seemed to be beyond Victoria at the moment. ''I . . . I must go home.''

''Why, you're white as new-sewn linen.'' Betty had

never seen her mistress in such a taking. "Come, the carriage is over here."

The maid helped her ladyship into the Harden coach, then called for the driver to hurry home. Victoria collapsed against the newly refurbished velvet squabs and stared bleakly out the window as the vehicle began the return journey back to Grosvenor Square.

Was it just the humiliation at discovering herself to be the subject of distasteful gossip that had wounded her heart so? Victoria knew it was far more. She could no longer deny what was in her heart. She'd fallen in love with Kit, while he appeared to be enamored by another woman. It was a woman's worse nightmare.

At first, all she could think was to get to the privacy of her own room, her misery was so great. But as the carriage slowed due to the heavy afternoon traffic, her mind returned to the conversation she'd held with her husband at the opera. He'd told her he would be much engaged with business and would be unable to be with the family. Why, he'd only used his work as an excuse so that he might cavort with some low woman.

Anger at the dawning revelation left her seething. Did he think she would be some shrinking mouse like her Aunt Vera who would allowed her husband to humiliate her before the whole of Society while she meekly turned her back and pretended such women didn't exist? Well her husband was about to find out otherwise if she had to track him all the way to that creature's very drawing room to find him.

CHAPTER TEN

Victoria marched into Cranford House with every intention of confronting her husband about his liaison with Lady Frey, but the sounds of raised voices echoed from above stairs into the foyer. She looked at the footman inquiringly as he took her hat and gloves.

" 'Tis Miss Harden and her cousin, my lady, in the Green Drawing Room."

Torn between her need to confront Kit and feeling it her duty to intercede between the tiresome pair, her personal ire won out. "Is my husband at home?"

"No, my lady, but he informed Mr. Matthews he would hopefully be joining the family for dinner this evening."

Victoria knew her anger was such that she could bide her time until then. So she hurried up the stairs and entered the Green Drawing Room. There she discovered Isabel and Paul standing toe to toe in the middle of the room glaring at one another. Young

Norman was seated in a chair near the fireplace observing the quarreling twosome as if they were a raree show.

"Whatever has occurred to get the pair of you at daggers drawn once again?" Victoria, her mind full of Kit's betrayal, was determined to put a quick end to the current contretemps between the cousins.

"Well you might ask, Lady Victoria, since you, like myself, thought that Cousin Isabel was resting in her room." Paul Harden turned to his hostess, but as he spoke he pointed an accusing finger at Miss Harden. "I just discovered this young lady out walking with the Marquis de Athier, as Norman and I came driving back from Soho."

Victoria sighed, "Isabel, what can you have been about?"

The young lady's chin rose. "I did not go out to meet the gentleman, if that is what you are all thinking. 'Tis only that I realized I needed something for my hair to match the yellow gown I am to wear this evening and went to buy ribbons. As I was leaving the shop, the marquis came along and offered to escort me home. My odious cousin is making such a fuss over nothing. I had a maid with me."

"That is not the point, Isabel. Your brother has made his wishes clear in regards to the marquis." Victoria suddenly wondered why she was bothering to concern herself with her husband's wishes when he took little interest in what any of them did. Had he not invited Paul to stay so that he might continue his dalliance with Lady Frey unimpeded? Anger burned anew in her.

Isabel sniffed. "That is only because a certain Prosing Provincial saw fit to interfere in my personal affairs and carry tales to Kit."

"I have only done what your brother asked, which is to keep you from falling into a scrape or creating a scandal. But alas, keeping a headstrong chit such as yourself out of trouble is a task more suited to a full regiment than to a single gentleman." Paul crossed his arms and glared at the young lady.

"You are insulting, sir, and I wish you to leave this house at once." Isabel turned her back on her cousin, causing her black curls to bounce and sway.

"Ha! You won't get rid of me that easily, my dear girl. I promised your brother to do a job and I'll see it through, no matter your wishing me at Jericho."

Isabel looked over her shoulder and gave a patently false smile. "Why, *dear cousin*, I would never wish you at Jericho. I believe Hades was the place that first came to my mind."

Victoria was about to reprimand her sister-in-law for her rudeness when Mr. Harden suddenly broke out in genuine laughter. "*Miss Harden*, one could never accuse you of being insipid or boring. Just unbelievably foolhardy and stubborn."

Victoria decided she'd best take Isabel in hand before the lady launched into a new round of insults. "My dear, I believe you are still overtired from all our late night revels. Perhaps you should retire to your room until you are feeling more the thing."

The young lady stood silent for several minutes, then she saw the look on Victoria's face and fathomed how completely she'd forgotten herself. After all, her cousin was a guest in their home, no matter how much she wished otherwise.

Isabel was certain her loss of dignity was all Cousin Paul's fault. His managing ways made her behave in the most absurd manner. But dear Victoria did not deserve to be caught in the middle after being so kind as to bring her to London. "I apologize for my conduct, dear Sister. As you suggested, I shall retire."

Without a backward glance at the gentleman who had started all the fuss, the lady exited the drawing room. Silence reigned in the room for several moments.

Noting Mr. Harden's frown as he stared at the closed door, Victoria said, "Sir, I do apologize for my sister-in-law's conduct. She—"

The gentleman put up his hand to stop her. "My dear Lady Victoria, you needn't apologize for my cousin. I have grown quite used to her verbal abuse. My only worry is that before she comprehends the marquis is all flash and no substance, she might foolishly take a step from which there is no return." Saying that, the gentleman excused himself and left the room.

Victoria looked at Norman. "I have grown positively weary trying to keep that pair from coming to blows."

Norman rose, a commiserative smile on his young face. "They do go at it like an epic battle between the Turks and the Greeks. I daresay, the difference is, the marquis shall have to sneak Cousin Isabel out of the house in a Trojan Horse, not in, if he truly wants the lady. My brother seems afraid she's contemplating a marriage over the anvil. But, for my part, I don't think Isabel is so foolish." The young man limped from the room.

Isabel eloping with the marquis! Victoria didn't see that happening. After all Miss Harden was no heiress and if the marquis was a fortune hunter, he would likely know that. But Isabel was full of all those foolish ideas garnered from the novels she read. An elopement might sound romantic to her, posed by a gentleman she imagined herself to love.

Victoria's gaze returned to the door through which Paul had disappeared. Was it possible that Mr. Harden had developed a *tendre* for his cousin? If so it was unfortunate, for Isabel had shown every indication that de Athier had captured her heart despite Kit's objections. Or was the green girl merely flattered to be pursued by a handsome, sophisticated gentleman?

In Victoria's mind there could be no comparison between the two men. Paul was hard-working, honest, likable and in a position to support a wife. The marquis was titled, but his situation was murky at best. No one seemed to have heard anything truly bad about the gentleman, only that he'd been a fixture in London for the past few years.

Unfortunately, where the ladies were concerned, the Frenchman was like a butterfly, handsome and brightly colorful, attracting a great deal of admiration. Victoria would liken Paul Harden to a moth, overlooked due to his modest appearance.

Victoria found herself so distracted by Isabel's affairs, that she'd reached her room before she again remembered she intended to confront Kit that very night about his dalliance with Lady Frey.

Kit waved the footman away as the man came forward to take his driving coat. He wouldn't be long at Cranford House, so there was no need to surrender the garment. He was more tired than he'd ever been, but he had an appointment with Lord Carew in scarcely an hour.

He'd intended the rare treat of sharing a meal with his family, but he'd been unduly detained driving Eve to Kingston-upon-Thames to view the famous wooden bridge with its twenty-two piers and twenty arches. The lady had claimed a strong desire to see the unique structure. Kit had spent the afternoon fielding her questions and in turn trying to charm her into relaxing her guard. But despite his best efforts he'd gleaned little information from the lady spy.

Curious, Kit inquired of the waiting footman, "Has the family dined, Martin?"

"They are at table now, sir."

Kit glanced at the case clock, and knew he didn't have time to change and he wasn't up to answering any questions from his mother about his absences. He dismissed the footman, deciding he would use what time he had, to rest in the library and gather his thoughts before his meeting.

As he was entering the large tome-filled room, he tossed his coat over the back of a chair, then poured himself a good measure of brandy before he went to his desk and sat down. Soon he became lost in thought while he sipped the amber liquid. He wasn't sure why, but instinct told him that Lady Frey was merely toying with him. She'd made little effort to conceal their liaison, which was the opposite to her former methods. In truth, while in public she was flirtatious and agreeable, always telling him her plans so that he might arrive at the same place. But the more he sidestepped her subtle questions, the more she seemed to resist him. She would graciously allow him to drive her home, but then plead fatigue at his request to come in for a brandy.

Kit was actually relieved he hadn't had to pretend to seduce the woman. It was all he could do each time he saw her, not to try to shake the information he wanted from her.

He closed his eyes, allowing his mind to drift to

the woman who occupied his thoughts nearly every moment. He hadn't seen Victoria in days. The memory of kissing her in her bedchamber drifted back and he felt a surge of passion. How he longed to teach his new bride more than the art of kissing. He envisioned himself trailing kisses down the curve of her delectable neck.

The viscount fell into a light sleep filled with dreams of his desirable wife, unaware that the lady, having learned of his return home had quietly entered the library.

Victoria noted that her husband sat dozing in his chair. She was struck by how boyish and defenseless he looked. Then she remembered why she'd come. He'd betrayed her trust and humiliated her. Some devilish imp seemed to take hold of her. Spying a book on a nearby table, she picked it up and slammed it down with a loud thump.

The viscount started from his sleep, spilling brandy down the front of his coat. "What the devil?" As he pulled out his handkerchief and began to pat the spill, he spied his wife, but there was no welcoming allure in those glittering green eyes as he'd seen in his dreams.

Her voice heavy with sarcasm, she inquired, "Do I now have your attention, my lord?"

"I would say you have gained the attention of half of Mayfair with that noise." Kit noted that Victoria looked enchanting in a pale green silk ball gown with a white lace overskirt, white roses nestled in the curls of her red hair. She was more desirable than ever. He couldn't resist grinning at his good fortune.

No answering smile curved his wife's lovely lips. Kit saw that the colour on her cheeks owed nothing to rouge. A rapid rise and fall of the shapely curve of her breasts above the low-cut bodice alerted him that she was extremely agitated. From the haughty look on her lovely face, he seemed to be the source of her agitation.

"What troubles you, my dear?"

"Don't call me that, sir. I have it on good authority that you have plainly exhibited to much of Society that I am not your dear," Victoria countered icily.

Kit looked down at the remaining brandy in his glass, swirling the liquid. He never showed by the least sign that her words froze his heart. He hoped his worst fears hadn't been realized and that the gossip hadn't reached Victoria. "What have you heard?"

"Your name being linked with Lady Frey's. Could you not have been a bit more discreet, sir, or was it your intention to deliberately humiliate me before Society?"

The wounded look in his wife's eyes made the decision to tell her everything easy. He wouldn't allow the dangerous game he was playing to jeopardize their future. She'd already proven he could trust her. "It is not what you think, my dear."

Her face was etched with disdain. "I may be an innocent in the ways of the world, my lord, but I am not naïve. You sir, are an unremitting cad to flaunt your mistress before the world. I have no doubt that my feelings are of little import, but what of your sister and mother? Must they, too, be put to the blush by the gossip?"

When she saw her husband put down his glass and come round the desk, Victoria took a step back, knowing that her body and heart might betray her mind. "Don't you—"

His hands closed on her arms, and he pulled her against him, giving her a hard kiss. Then in a husky voice, he demanded, "Listen to me, Victoria. I have not betrayed you. I am not having an affair with Lady Frey."

Before she could respond, he drew her to a chair by the fire and forced her to sit down, then knelt in front of her blocking her escape from his explanation. "I insist you listen. You must believe what I am now about to tell you and swear you won't repeat a single word outside this room, not to my mother or sister, not to anyone."

The lady looked doubtful, but she scanned his face for several seconds, then nodded her head in agreement.

"If you will remember, I never spoke about what occurred in Portugal after I left you. My mission was secret and urgent. I was to meet a man named Sir James Marks at an inn near the Spanish border. To make a long story short, it was a trap. When I arrived, James had already been shot by the French and was dying." Kit's face reflected much of his pain at what he was telling her.

Victoria gasped, her green eyes grew wide and she reached out her hand to his. "How terrible."

He took her slender white fingers and entwined them with his. He quickly told her what the baronet had said about a spy operating in London to betray the network of men who worked gathering information. Then about returning home and learning from Lord Carew, the man for whom he worked at Horse Guards, that Lady Frey was the person they suspected.

"An Englishwoman spying for the French? Why would she do such a horrid thing?" There was part of Victoria which despised the woman for betraying her country. Still, the idea of a female engaging herself in the passing of government secrets planted a seed of awe in Victoria.

"I do not know that she is English for certain. I suspect that one of her parents might have been French. Unfortunately, despite all the time I have wasted pursuing her, I have learned little. More importantly, I've been unable to discover the name of the man with whom we know she is working. That is why she hasn't been arrested and why I'm still pursuing her." Kit watched as Victoria nodded, then fell silent. Thinking that she still doubted his story, he slid his arms around her and drew her down to the floor on her knees so that they were facing one another.

"Victoria, I have regretted every minute away from here, from you. Have no doubt I want to honour my marriage vows." To prove his statement, he crushed her to him, then captured her tempting mouth with demanding mastery. He was delighted when he felt her tentative response grow to hungry need.

The blood begin to pound through his veins and Kit knew if he didn't stop now, he would scandalize the entire staff by taking his wife before the library fire. Reluctantly he pulled away from her, but reveled in the unfulfilled desire he detected in her eyes. He'd managed to ignite a spark which he was certain would flame into full passion when he was free to seek his heart's desire.

A knock sounded at the door, causing Kit to grin at Victoria. He rose and helped her to her feet, then called for the visitor to enter. He observed his wife turning from the entering servant, trying to regain her wits. The footman carried a tray with a message.

Kit broke the seal, quickly scanning the missive. "I must leave at once. There is urgent news."

Victoria stepped forward and clutched his hands. "Lady Frey's accomplice, you think him French."

Kit shook his head. "There is no way of knowing, my dear. There is many a man who would betray his country for enough gold. That is why you must be wary of all strangers at the moment. I don't think you need worry, but there is always the possibility that this spy may try to get information about my activities from you, Isabel or *Mamãe*."

"You asked Paul here to watch over and protect us from this spy," Victoria said with dawning realization, then she blushed at all the unkind thoughts she'd had about her husband for introducing his cousin into the household.

"He knows the whole story."

Kit reluctantly drew his hand from Victoria's then walked over and draped his driving cape about his shoulders. He glanced back to where Victoria stood. "Am I forgiven, my dear?"

"Only if you will promise to keep no more such secrets from me. I should far rather know, than be left to think the worst." Victoria, still trembling from the depths of the passions he'd so recently stirred in her, watched her husband. She wanted to be a part of everything in his life.

He came back to where she stood near the desk. Taking her in his arms, he passionately kissed her. "It should soon be over, but I shall always try to tell you the truth. Promise that you will not worry. There is little danger to me, since I know what I am facing. Go to the ball this evening and hold your head high. Ignore the gossip. I promise that when this is over I shall make it up to you by taking you on a honeymoon trip."

As Kit moved to the door, Victoria called, "Take care."

He grinned at her reassuringly then exited the library, leaving his wife as agitated as she'd been upon entering the chamber, but for an entirely different reason. She moved back to the chair near the fire and sat, staring into the flames, her mind full of all he'd told her. Regardless of his assurances, she was certain his mission was not lacking in danger. If only she could do something to help him, but Lady Frey would obviously avoid Victoria, thinking her nothing more than a jealous wife. She hated feeling so powerless to protect the man she loved.

She suddenly realized that, for all his passion, he still hadn't said those words she longed to hear. Did he love her? He'd said he wanted to honor his vows, but that was hardly the same thing. Still, his kisses had given her hope that once he'd completed this business he would return to her.

She heard Luisa and Isabel in the hall, ready to leave for the ball. Victoria knew she must gather her wits and join them. With a decided lack of enthusiasm, she left to begin her night's entertainment.

Kit hurried down the dark street. Despite the urgency of his mission, his mind kept returning to the embrace in the library. Victoria had felt wonderful in his arms.

"My lord, over here." A voice sounded in the darkness.

Kit halted and realized he was across the street from Lady Frey's house. The Bow Street Runner stepped from a darkened doorway, and motioned the viscount to step away from the light of the oil streetlamp.

"What is happening, Grafton?"

"Looks like our little pigeon is about to take flight within the next day or so, sir."

Kit turned again to look at the house, but he could see nothing of an unusual nature, as light poured from the drawing room window. "Why do you think she is about to flee? All looks quiet."

"Aye, it does, but two lads have been removing bits of furniture since sunset. I trailed 'em to a fourgon at the end of the street. Fell into conversation with 'em, right innocent like, and they say the furniture is bein' sold. But one of the fellows was flirtin' with the lady's maid and she seemed to think Lady Frey is goin' on a journey by week's end."

Kit swore softly. He would have to tell Lord Carew. They couldn't permit Eve and her accomplice to escape. The pair had cost England too many good men to be allowed to slip away to France without paying for their crimes.

Kit told the runner to keep watch and no matter the time of day or night, to summon him if the lady looked as if she were leaving. He'd chase her all the way to Paris if he had to. She was going to pay for betraying England.

"Good heavens, Victoria. Your wits are positively to let this evening." Luisa eyed her daughter-in-law curiously as they stood at the edge of the dance floor at Lady Willingham's ball.

"I do apologize for my distraction. What were you saying, madam?" Victoria came out of her brown study and made an effort to listen to the dowager.

"I merely observed that the marquis appears quite

enamored with Isabel. I think he might come up to scratch, as the English so vulgarly say, this very week.''

Victoria's gaze flew to the pair who were now dancing. "But, my dear lady, do you not realize that Kit has expressly forbidden his sister to encourage the gentleman? Any offer by the marquis will be refused, I feel certain.''

"Bah!" The dowager waved her hand dismissively. "Lady Forester said we would be fools to whistle down a title, no matter a French one, for an overly large girl like Isabel. I shall speak with my son. Dear Agnes says she would have no qualms about allowing a daughter of hers to form an alliance with the gentleman.''

"Lady Forester has no daughter or son." Nor common sense, as far as Victoria could see, if the lady was encouraging Luisa to condone an alliance with a gentleman who, despite his time in Society, was a mystery.

The dowager, having no response for Victoria's logic, changed the subject. "Pray, who is that very corpulent gentleman, the one who everyone is making such a fuss about?" The dowager pointed with her fan at a party that had just entered the ballroom, led by the gentleman in question.

Victoria's eyes widened for just a moment. Like most in Society she was not immune to the excitement of celebrity. "I do believe that is our new Regent, the Prince of Wales.''

"That great hulking walrus is the so-called First Gentleman of Europe? No doubt because he is always first at table." Luisa's scornful gaze raked the large prince up and down as the gentleman made conversation with his particular lady friends.

Victoria struggled not to smile. "Despite his love

of fine food, I do believe he is considered quite charming and to have excellent taste in all things.''

"I can only say, he is not my idea of a gentleman who is pleasing.'' The dowager looked around and used her fan to indicate several men on the far side of the ballroom. "Look there, beside those palms. Baron Waldron and the Comte d'Caille are most pleasing to the feminine eye.'' The taller of the well-dressed gentlemen, seeing the gesture by the lady raised a hand in acknowledgement, then spoke to the man beside him and they began to make their way towards the ladies.

Victoria felt excited as she surveyed the approaching *comte*, whose name she'd heard only this afternoon linked to Lady Frey. As the gentleman came nearer, Victoria guessed him to be in his forties, tall and slender. His dark hair was artfully brushed to disguise a thinning near the front. His face was mildly lined, but decidedly handsome with pale grey eyes and full smiling lips. He was elegantly dressed in a dark brown coat with white waistcoat and knee breeches. A large diamond was nestled into an intricate cravat. The dowager was indeed correct that he was pleasing to the eye.

But Victoria's thoughts were going in an entirely different direction. Might this be the man Kit was searching for? Or had he merely been a diversion for the lady, to protect the real spy's identity? Either way, Victoria was certain there could be no harm in her engaging the gentleman in a little innocent conversation at the ball.

The Frenchman bowed deeply over Luisa's hand, making her blush like a young girl. "*Bonsoir, madame. You are as lovely as ever and may my friend, Waldron,* and I request an introduction to your lovely companion?''

"My dear Victoria, allow me to present Lord Waldron and the Comte d'Caille who are dear friends of Lady Forester. My daughter-in-law, Lady Victoria.''

The baron bowed a greeting, but the Frenchman took her hand and pressed a kiss on the gloved surface. "*Enchanté*, my lady.''

Victoria said all that was proper to the gentlemen, but her mind was rushing about searching for a way to get the *comte* alone. Spying several sets of double doors on the opposite side of the ballroom which had been opened onto a garden to release the heat of the numerous candles and the press of bodies, she decided to use a decidedly feminine trick.

She opened her fan and began to ply it vigorously. '' 'Tis quite a crush, is it not, sir?'' She addressed her comment directly to the *comte*, as Luisa and the baron had fallen into conversation about their mutual dislike of balls, each preferring card parties.

A twinkle came into the Frenchman's grey eyes, as if he knew how to properly play the game, and he bowed. "*Madame*, allow me to escort you to the terrace where I believe you will soon feel better. *N'est-ce pas?*"

"An excellent suggestion, sir." Victoria excused herself from her mother-in-law who eyed her curiously, then allowed the *comte* to lead her around the dancing couples towards the cool night air.

"I believe your husband is heir to the Duke of Townsend's excessively fine stables, no?"

Victoria saw no reason to go into the estrangement between Kit and his grandfather, instead she turned the subject back to the *comte*. "Are you one of those gentleman who think of nothing but their horses, sir? And here I thought I had made a conquest, but you want only to hear about the duke's stables." They stepped through the open doors onto the terrace.

"I admire many things, Lady Ridgecrest. Fine horses, beautiful ladies—beautiful ladies riding fine horses."

Victoria was struck with an idea. He'd given her an opportunity to arrange a further meeting with him. One which would engender less comment than a prolonged walk in a dark garden. "I do so like to ride horses, sir. In fact, I ride every morning precisely at ten in the Park."

"And would a gentleman such as myself be a welcomed addition to your ride?"

"To be sure, sir."

She looked up just then to see Paul coming through the terrace door like an avenging angel.

"Dear Lady Victoria, I find you at last. I am afraid we must cut our evening short, for Cousin Isabel is not feeling up to snuff." Mr. Harden glowered at d'Caille.

Victoria barely had time to say a farewell, before Paul grabbed her arm and swept her off the moonlit terrace. As they re-entered the ballroom, leaving the *comte* behind, Kit's cousin hissed in Victoria's ear, "Is it not bad enough that I have Cousin Isabel setting her cap for that French man-milliner without you casting out lures to that old Paris *roué*? Must I remind you that you have a husband?"

Victoria stopped in her tracks. Angrily she faced the seething Mr. Harden. "Don't be ridiculous, sir, I was trying to help my husband by getting information from that gentleman who was Lady Frey's last . . . liaison."

Paul's brows rose. "For the love of heaven, don't involve yourself in his affairs. 'Tis too dangerous for a woman, Lady Victoria. Leave matters to Kit. Besides, we've one Frenchman too many lurking around the Hardens' without adding another.'' He then turned and stalked off, looking to gather up the remaining members of the family to depart.

Victoria knew it was no use to argue with the gentleman. But as she followed him from the ballroom, she decided she would not be so easily dissuaded. She was certain she might be able to do something to help Kit and saw no reason to wait meekly at home. After all, she would be with d'Caille in a very public place. There was little danger and the Frenchman might well tell her something which could help Kit. The *comte* would meet her in Hyde Park the following morning and she fully intended to go.

CHAPTER ELEVEN

Victoria positioned the low-crowned brown beaver hat over her red curls at a slight angle, then observed the effect, along with her new habit in the mirror. She liked the russet velvet she'd chosen for the high-waisted garment and the amber ruffle of silk which brushed under her chin as well as the twin rows of gold buttons on the short jacket. She knew the simple lines flattered her and she wished she was dressing for a ride with Kit, but she'd heard him leave early that morning.

A twinge of guilt tugged at her conscience. Her husband was likely to disapprove of her plan to meet with d'Caille as much as Paul had disliked her walking on the terrace with the Frenchman. She pushed the worry from her mind, reminding herself that all would be forgiven should she discover any information from the *comte*.

About to pick up her crop, she halted when a knock

sounded at the door. Isabel looked around the wooden portal as soon as Victoria called, "Come."

"Oh, I did not know you intended to ride this morning." Miss Harden appeared disappointed.

Victoria looked at the clock on the mantelpiece and realized she had plenty of time before she was to meet the *comte* and clearly Isabel wanted to talk privately or she wouldn't have come to Victoria's room. "Was there something you needed, my dear?"

The young lady wandered over to the window and looked out, then gave a large sigh. "I was just speaking with *Mamãe* at breakfast. She says I would be a complete goose to refuse the marquis's proposal of marriage if he comes up to scratch. She reminded me that I have no other serious suitors." The young lady looked at her sister-in-law, a marked bleakness in her dark eyes. "But I do not want to marry the gentleman."

Victoria went to Isabel and took her hands, drawing her down on the sofa near the window. "I do not think your brother will permit the gentleman to pay his addresses to you. So I don't think you need worry about your mother's wishes in regard to the marquis."

A look of relief settled on Miss Harden's face. "I am glad. He is very handsome and amiable, but . . ." she paused before adding, "he does not make my heart flutter the way the ladies' hearts do upon meeting the hero in the novels I read. Do you understand, for I am certain *Mamãe* does not?"

Having experienced that very sensation a great deal in the presence of her husband, Victoria was certain she knew what Isabel referred to. She merely nodded her head. "Then why ever have you been encouraging the marquis at every turn?"

Isabel bit at her lower lip, then looked sheepishly

at Victoria. "I wouldn't have, only Mr. Harden said such cutting things about my choice in gentleman. I suddenly felt the need to defend the marquis and prove to my cousin that I was quite able to handle my own affairs."

"Good heavens, my dear. Don't encourage just any gentleman merely to spite your cousin. Marriage is for a lifetime and your cousin will be back home in Essex in a matter of weeks."

The young lady gave another large sigh. " 'Tis not like there have been all that many suitors to encourage." Isabel ran her hands down over her ample hips. "It seems I am not to the gentlemen's taste. Whatever shall I do if no one offers for me this Season?"

Victoria patted the young lady's hand. "Why, then we shall come to Town the following Season. After all, my dear, you are but eighteen. You have years to find a gentleman who can make your heart behave in the proper manner the novelists exalt."

Isabel laughed delightedly. "Oh, Victoria, you are quite the finest thing to happen to our family since we came to England." She then gave her sister-in-law a kiss, and rose, going to the door. "I mustn't keep you from your ride."

As the lady departed, Victoria gathered her gloves and riding crop, wondering if her husband agreed with his sister's feelings about her. She made her way downstairs, and within minutes a groom was in front of the town house with one of the mares Victoria had purchased upon arriving in Town. A feeling of nervous anticipation raced through her as she urged her horse towards Hyde Park.

She was surprised at the scarcity of riders as she and her groom entered the Park. Thinking herself a bit early, she put her horse into a gentle trot and rode away from the main path to the far side of the Serpentine, then drew to a halt. From there she could observe the other riders trotting up and down Rotten Row. When she spied the *comte* she would join him.

She hadn't seen Kit since he'd revealed his mission in the library the previous evening. Victoria began to wonder about the urgent message he'd received. Had they already caught the man who was helping Lady Frey? Was she wasting her time waiting for the *comte*?

She heard the rapid beat of hooves and looked around to see the Frenchman approaching her in her remote locality. Suddenly she wished she'd not isolated herself so far from the other riders. After all, this gentleman might just be the spy Kit sought.

The *comte*, however, looked anything but sinister. He was properly dressed in a green riding coat and buff buckskins, his beaver hat set at a rakish angle over his handsome countenance. He drew his horse beside hers then rose in the stirrups and bowed, a wickedly seductive smile on his handsome face. "Ah, *ma chérie*, such a delight to see you this fine morning."

Lord Carew sat back in his chair and eyed Christopher across the white tablecloth of his dining room. He'd invited Ridgecrest to breakfast to discuss the current state of affairs in the Frey matter and they'd spent the whole of the meal planning their next move. But now the earl had one final thing to tell the viscount. He was uncertain how his young subordinate and friend would take the news he was about to impart.

He cleared his throat, then announced, "I received an important dispatch from Portugal today from General Murray." The earl was referring to the quartermaster general in charge of Wellington's exploring officers, the young soldiers who gathered intelligence against the French.

Kit put down his coffee cup. "His men captured something important?"

The earl nodded. "I fear your days of working in Portugal are over, my boy. It is no longer safe." Carew opened a leather pouch and drew out a large square of paper showing signs it had been folded, and pushed it across the linen surface.

Kit took the document and turned the paper around, discovering a passable drawing of himself, perhaps a little more sinister than in actuality, but the French artist had captured a reasonable likeness. The words *Le Fantôme Anglais* were inscribed under the picture along with an offer of fifty gold ducats for his capture. Kit glanced up at the earl.

"Several copies of these have been found on captured or dead soldiers. I fear your French colonel in Campo Mayor was no fool and he is determined to get his hands on you again."

Kit realized that his tenure as a British agent had ended with that picture, anonymity being essential for such a secret mission. But he felt merely a twinge of disappointment. Not only had he grown tired of the life, but his circumstances had altered. He was married now, and it was a surprise how much that meant to him, considering it was a state he hadn't sought. "So my usefulness to you is at an end, sir."

"Not at all, my boy. We must bring this spy business to a satisfactory conclusion then I should like your assistance here in London in the future. You know Portugal, Christopher. You can help prepare new agents for what to expect before I send them over."

Somehow that seemed appropriate. He could now

begin a proper marriage with Victoria and still do something to assist his country in its time of war. "I should like that, sir."

The old gentleman pointed at the drawing. "Keep that. You might want to show it to your sons years from now and tell them tales about what you did to help defeat Bonaparte."

Kit nodded his head and smiled. The idea of a settled life at Harwick with Victoria and children looked very appealing.

The gentlemen said their farewells. Kit promised to inform the earl should Lady Frey attempt to flee or if he was able to find the name of her accomplice.

It was still early as Kit maneuvered his carriage down Upper Brook Street, but traffic was far heavier than when he'd first traveled to Lord Carew's. He couldn't wait to inform Victoria that he would no longer be leaving on dangerous missions in the Peninsula. Entering Grosvenor Square, he tooled his curricle around the fenced green, his thoughts on how his wife would smile when he gave her the news.

Almost as if his contemplation had conjured her up, Victoria, on the opposite side of the square and looking elegant in a fashionable brown riding habit, rode away from Cranford House as she headed in the direction of Hyde Park. Thinking he would like nothing better than to take her up with him and drive in the Park, he determined to overtake her. He would have her groom return her horse to the stable, and he might spend an enjoyable few moments undisturbed with the lady before he returned to his government affairs.

But a horse and rider could move easier through the busy morning traffic than a carriage, and he soon lost her in the crowded street. Unconcerned, he drove to the Park, knowing he would find her there.

Kit put his cattle into an unfashionable canter as he entered Hyde Park, hoping to overtake Victoria somewhere along the Row. He wasn't certain what drew his attention to the site, but as he glanced to his left he saw a pair seated on horseback on the opposite side of the Serpentine. At once he identified the bright curls of his wife under a dashing brown hat, then his gaze narrowed as he realized she was with the Comte d'Caille, one of London's most notorious rakes.

A black rage filled him to think that someone of the *comte*'s ilk had Victoria so nearly in his clutches. Kit's hands immediately tightened on the reins and he turned his curricle so quickly that Lord Rumfield, a noted whip who drove out every morning, had to veer his phaeton off the path to avoid a collision. But Kit was oblivious to the string of oaths filling the air behind him, he was so intent on getting to his wife.

He didn't blame Victoria for having been drawn into an unseemly meeting with the old roué, after all, she was an innocent in the way of Society. Paul had warned him last night that keeping watch over three ladies was more of a task than one gentleman could reliably handle, especially when two of the ladies were a bit headstrong and were wont to go their own way.

If Victoria had been naïvely lured into an assignation, Kit had only himself to blame for being too involved with other affairs. She was a beautiful, desirable woman who, if seen to be ignored by her husband, would attract hardened rakes like d'Caille. Might his innocent young wife have fallen under such a man's spell?

The idea that he could lose her heart to another made him feel like someone had struck him. In a flash of astounding enlightenment, Kit realized that this woman's love meant more to him than his life. His world would have little meaning without the knowledge that Victoria was his, body and soul. There was no longer a feeling of being duty-bound to this marriage. He didn't just desire her, he loved her and wanted to protect her.

Relief flooded through him as he spied Victoria's groom waiting unobtrusively by a stand of trees. Even a scoundrel like the *comte* wouldn't try anything untoward, with a servant as witness. Kit drove his carriage as close as he safely could to the riders' horses. Two pairs of guilty eyes turned in his direction, but within a matter of seconds, Victoria's face was filled with genuine delight and she called, "Kit, I had not thought to see you here." Her tone warmed his heart.

The *comte*'s brow's rose only briefly as he watched Lady Victoria's husband maneuver his carriage to within inches of their horses. He sidled his animal away from the lady and tipped his hat with a polite, "My lord." It was never his policy to dally with ladies who possessed jealous husbands.

Kit gave the gentleman a curt nod, but addressed his wife. "My dear, I was hoping you would join me in the carriage this fine morning. Your groom can return your horse to Cranford House."

Victoria didn't wait for assistance in dismounting. She excused herself to the *comte*, slid deftly from her horse, and led the animal to the waiting groom before hurrying over to gratefully grasp her husband's hand as he assisted her into his curricle.

With a second nod and a narrowing of his eyes meant to issue a warning to the *comte*, Kit set his curricle in motion. He was very aware of her presence beside him, and he suddenly wished that Lord Carew, Lady Frey, and her accomplice were all in the distant past as he drove quickly away from the Frenchman. He was still awed by the realization that he had fallen so totally in love with her.

Too relieved to have his wife away from the rake to do anything more, he only mildly chided her. "My dear, I know you are unused to the ways of Society, but you mustn't allow such an unsavory gentleman to lure you out for a morning ride."

"He is a shocking libertine, no doubt, but I must own that I was the one who arranged the assignation, sir."

Kit hauled on the reins in such a manner that he nearly threw his wife into the dirt. "You did what?"

Straightening her hat, Victoria turned to her husband. "I was trying to help you."

"Help me, by involving yourself with that rakehell? Did the cad take liberties? Must I call him out?"

Victoria's green eyes grew quite round and she put her hand upon his arm. "Not that, Kit. I would never forgive myself if you were drawn into a duel because I merely tried to get information from him. He was quite harmless and most unhelpful, preferring to speak about my eyes in the most absurd manner."

Kit liked the feel of her long slender fingers clutching his arm. As her nearness stirred the blood in his loins, he found it difficult to concentrate. "Get information? What information?"

With a shrug of her shoulders, Victoria tried to explain. "I thought that since Lady Frey was so good at gathering information, I might be able to find if the *comte* was her accomplice."

Her words seemed to penetrate his desire-fogged

brain. Despite the reins in his hands, he suddenly took her arms, and drew her to him. The horses shifted back and forth, unclear about the commands the leather straps carried from the impassioned driver. "My dear naïve Victoria, d'Caille is no more a spy than Prinny is a soldier, despite all his fancy uniforms. I couldn't bear it should you get drawn into this dangerous business. Something might well happen to you. Promise me you won't try your hand playing at lady spy again."

Victoria grabbed the back of the curricle seat as the vehicle rocked about with the confused cattle, her lips pursed in a defiant way. "I don't see why I shouldn't—"

Kit couldn't resist. He captured her defiant mouth, kissing her with a heated ravishment better suited to a bedchamber than the open fields of the Park. But his cattle, having had their reins tugged, then slack, then jerked back and forth, decided they were being requested to trot off. They set out at a crisp pace straight towards the Serpentine River.

Thrown against the leather squabs of the curricle by the sudden motion, the couple were jarred apart then fell to laughing. Kit tightened his grip on the reins, bringing the horses back to a gentle walk and turning them back to the path. "I think we might want to continue this in the privacy of Cranford House at some later time, my love, before we cool our ardor in the river."

Victoria blushed at his words, then laughed at the image of them, carriage and all bobbing in the water.

"As to the other, I want you to promise you won't try to inquire into Eve Frey's affairs on your own. 'Tis too dangerous."

Engulfed in a state of supreme happiness at her

husband's kiss and declaration, Victoria smiled then docilely stated, "I promise, Kit."

He drove back to Grosvenor Square, all the while making small talk so that his wife might regain her composure before again facing the servants and his family. He needed the time as well to rein in his desire to take her straight upstairs upon their return.

When they arrived home, the town house seemed unusually quiet for that hour of the day. Kit inquired as to where everyone had gone. Matthews, who removed his lordship's driving cape, informed them that the dowager was out making morning calls, Miss Harden had left with her maid to visit Hookham's Library, Mr. Norman was at the British Museum and Mr. Harden had left without informing anyone of his destination.

Kit looked at his beautiful wife, thinking he would make a very scandalous proposition about how they should finish the remainder of the morning since they were quite alone save the servants.

"My lord, a message arrived for you earlier." The butler retrieved the letter from a nearby table and handed it to his master, having no clue that the viscount suddenly wished him to perdition.

Kit impatiently broke the seal and read the missive. Eve requested he call at Half Moon Street as soon as possible. Filled with a sense of hope that he might at last put an end to this matter, he folded the note and placed it into his pocket. With a smile for Victoria, he excused himself. "I cannot ignore this letter, my dear. I think matters are near an end. I don't know when I shall return, but don't worry."

He kissed her hand, his eyes telling her he wanted to kiss much more were it not for the servant beside them, then he retrieved his coat from Matthews and left.

Victoria climbed the stairs on a cloud of euphoria. Her husband had called her his love and declared he couldn't bear losing her. He seemed to think his mission was near its end. It looked as if all her dreams might come true.

Victoria had just finished changing into a yellow jaconet muslin, scalloped at the feet and bordered at the wrist and collar with white brocade ribbons, when an urgent knock sounded at her door. Before she could utter a word, the visitor entered the room.

Luisa's face was ghostly pale as she hurried to her daughter-in-law. The black lace had slipped from her mantilla and was bunched around her neck. A pool of tears glistened in her dark eyes. "The most dreadful thing has occurred, my dear."

Victoria took the dowager by the hand and led her to a sofa, her heart pounding, worried that something terrible had happened to Kit. "Whatever is the matter, dear lady?"

Lady Ridgecrest collapsed on the sofa, then babbled for several moments in rapid Portuguese to a baffled Victoria. Realizing her mistake, the dowager apologized and returned to English. "I said that dreadful Duke of Townsend is in London."

Relief flooded Victoria and she felt a sudden desire to shake her mother-in-law for having given her such a scare, but in truth the lady knew not that her son was involved in such perilous matters. "Why should that be of concern to us? Kit is not dependent on His Grace for our needs. I fear you have allowed old hurts to shatter your nerves."

The dowager shook her head. "Dear Agnes says that Townsend never visits Town during the Season. And Mrs. Whatley thinks he's arrived because he heard we are here. I am certain he has come to again slander me as he did all those years ago. We shall be forced to return home to Harwick in disgrace."

The circumstances of His Grace's sudden appearance were indeed peculiar, but Victoria found it hard to believe that he still harbored ill feelings after all this time. Unfortunately, Luisa's new friends seemed to be fanning her worst fears to a frenzy. Never having met the duke, Victoria had little inkling into his opinions and motives, so she concentrated on soothing her mother-in-law's sensibilities. "I am certain we have made sufficient friends over the course of our visit that we need not fear being given the cut direct due to the duke's disapproval."

Luisa rose and began to pace. "You don't understand. I am Portuguese. I have been looked down upon on account of my foreign birth, by everyone from servants to the neighbors. It has been very difficult for me since coming to your country. These few weeks in Town have been the first time I've ever felt truly welcomed in England."

At last Victoria understood a great deal about her mother-in-law. The lady took every incident which thwarted her wishes and made it a personal affront to her heritage. The string of fired servants and the failure to socialize with her neighbors at Harwick could all be laid at the duke's door for his rejection of his daughter-in-law all those years ago.

Rising, Victoria went to Luisa. "Come, let me take you to your room. I am certain that once you lie down and rest you will remember all the friends you have made and know they would not abandon you simply for fear of offending some gentleman who rarely comes to Town, duke or no.''

The lady's face lightened at that. She allowed Victoria to lead her back to her room where she settled in her bed with curtains drawn and soon forgot her fears amid talk of the future engagements they planned to attend.

Over an hour later, Victoria was able to leave her mother-in-law to rest. She was quite worn out from entertaining the lady, but had finally convinced Luisa they would not be snubbed even if His Grace had come to create mischief, which Victoria doubted was his motive.

She wandered down to the front hall and discovered a letter from her cousin Charles in the post. She went into the library to read his news. To her delight, the captain informed her that Dona Ines had consented to be his wife and they were to be married at month's end before he rejoined his regiment. Just as she was folding the letter with the intention of returning to her room, a vigorous knocking sounded at the front door. She heard a footman open the door and a voice call, ''I've an urgent message from a Mr. Paul Harden for the viscountess.''

The man's tone told Victoria something was seriously wrong. She went to the door and called, ''Martin, send him to the library.''

The messenger stepped into the room carrying the smell of the stables with him. Victoria was certain he was a groom or ostler from some local inn, and wondered what had happened to Paul. ''I am Lady Ridgecrest.''

The lad pulled a battered hat from his brown hair and gave a clumsy bow, then extended a crumpled note to her. ''Name's Sam Green and I work at the

White Dove." Seeing the puzzled look on the lady's face he added, " 'Tis an inn on the road to Dover, my lady. The gentleman gave me a half-crown to brin' this to you and promised there'd be another one from you if I could make it to here by twelve o'clock."

Victoria couldn't imagine what Paul was doing on the road to Dover since his estate lay north of London. And what was the urgency, for the clock showed the time wanting five minutes to the hour. She found a small pouch in the desk and paid the young man. She thanked him for his speedy delivery, then sent him on his way. She broke the seal and quickly read the words then gasped.

> *Find Kit at once. de Athier abducted Isabel from the street near the town house for some nefarious purpose other than marriage. The carriage is fleeing for the coast and I follow. I shall try to leave a message at the Black Knight in Dover if time allows. Paul*

Kit's worse nightmare had been realized. The marquis must be the spy and he'd taken Isabel to force Kit to reveal what he knew. There was no time to waste, but Victoria hadn't a clue as to where Kit had gone, and Paul needed help now.

Then she was struck with a horrifying idea. What if the marquis had abducted Kit as well? The thought tore at her insides. She couldn't lose the man she loved now.

With great effort she reined in her rampant imagination. Kit might have merely been lured to Lady Frey's house so that Isabel could be taken. She prayed that was the case.

Either way, there appeared to be only one solution. She would see if Kit was with Lady Frey. If he wasn't she would go after Isabel herself. With her father's pistol, she could be as menacing to the marquis or his accomplice as any man. The decision was one she was certain her husband would object to but there was no one else she could turn to for help. Norman Harden was just a boy and, while the Duke of Townsend was in Town, he hadn't taken the least interest in his family. She wouldn't waste valuable time trying to convince him to do the right thing.

Having settled the matter in her mind, that she was doing the only thing she could, Victoria wrote a vague note to explain both her and Isabel's absence to Lady Ridgecrest. She left the missive with Martin to be delivered when the dowager arose, then she ordered a horse to be saddled for a gentleman and brought round for her. The footman's mouth gaped open for a moment, but Victoria ignored his shocked countenance and hurried upstairs to change.

CHAPTER TWELVE

Several people shouted their opinion of the young cawker who barreled through the streets of London at breakneck speed on a grey mare, thinking him some rude halfling new to Town. The rider ignored the yells and bent lower over the animal to urge the horse to go faster, which caused his overlarge drab cape to billow up like the arms of a wraith.

Victoria had made free use of young Norman Harden's apparel, he being only slightly taller than her. It had helped that he was away from the house at that moment and unable to protest her intrusion into his bedchamber. The attire, unlike her former disguise, did little to hide her feminine curves, so she'd donned a cape to cover her improper rig.

She entered Half Moon Street at a gallop, and was about to slow her horse to inquire of a passerby which residence belonged to Lady Frey, when she spied Kit's curricle drawn up in front of a white house. She reined the animal behind the vehicle being held by a young lad, no doubt one of Lady Frey's servants, and hopped down. The boy watched her tie her horse to the rear of the curricle, without making any comment. She dashed up the steps and rapped the brass knocker sharply against the black door.

The maid who answered the summons eyed the visitor curiously, thinking the young man with the red curls and delicate face under the wide-brimmed hat a bit too foppish for her taste. Remembering her instructions, she intoned, "Lady Frey is not home to visitors."

To her amazement the frail-looking gentleman, without so much as removing his hat, pushed her aside and stepped into the hall, first staring into the two rooms which opened off the foyer. Upon discovering them empty, he dashed up the stairs. "Hey there! What are you doin', sir? I told you . . ."

Victoria scarcely heard the maid, she was so intent on finding Kit. She tried the first door at the landing, but found it to be an empty sewing room. She hurried to the next one at the rear of the hall as she heard the protesting maid coming up the stairs.

She stepped into a small drawing room that reeked of perfume. There stood Lady Frey at a small rosewood table, dressed in a frilly pink negligee which barely concealed her shapely curves, pouring wine into glasses. The widow looked up and frowned. "Who the devil are you? Get out of my house at once or I shall have you thrown out."

Kit's brows rose when he turned to see his wife again dressed like a young gentleman in pantaloons, coat and driving cape. Something was wrong for Victoria to be here in this manner. "What has happened?"

"De Athier abducted Isabel and is on his way to

Dover. Paul has gone after her. He requested you come at once."

Fury nearly choked him. He turned his dark gaze on Eve. He'd played her little game long enough. Two steps brought him to stand in front of her. He grasped her arms and shook her. "Where has he taken my sister?"

Eve Frey's face flushed. "Unhand me, sir. I know nothing of this de Athier. Why would you think I should have any knowledge of your silly sister and her amorous dalliances?"

His anger was so great, he gave little thought to her being a woman. Despite being a woman, she was responsible for the death of four agents. He'd been lulled into a false feeling that there was little danger since he knew her for what she was. But the lady and her accomplice had struck where he was most vulnerable. They had abducted his sister. He shoved her away from him in disgust. She stumbled and fell backward onto an Egyptian sofa.

A small brown flask flew from the pocket of her wrapper and tumbled off the sofa to the rug. Kit stared at the bottle, knowing that it had been intended for him. "Poison or laudanum?"

Eve clutched the front of her warper, then defiantly sniffed, "I had the headache last night and my maid brought it to me. I put the potion in my pocket and forgot about it. 'Tis only mild sleeping drops."

Kit watched as Victoria picked up the bottle, uncorked it and took a sniff. "Laudanum."

He took the bottle from her, then came to the sofa to tower over Eve Frey. "I should say there is enough here to put one to sleep permanently. Unless you tell me exactly what de Athier's plan was, madam, I shall save England the expense of a rope by pouring every drop down your traitorous throat."

Lady Frey eyes grew wide and her trembling hand came up to hover in front of her mouth in a protective gesture. She stuttered out, "N-no gentleman would harm a lady."

"You are no lady, you are a French spy. Where has the marquis taken my sister?"

There was clearly something in his tone which told Eve that he would make good on his threat. "René took her to White Lily Cottage just north of Dover. I was to drug you and bring you there by this evening. He was certain you would tell the names of all the agents to save her life."

Kit stood menacingly over the woman, his fingers still clutching the stopper of the flask. He remained thus so long that Victoria came to him and gently removed the bottle from his hand and dropped it in her pocket, fearful that he might make good on his threat, his anger at the lady was so great. "You must leave at once to save your sister."

He looked at her as if he'd just wakened from a trance. He nodded his head. "But first I must make certain our Lady Frey is not left unattended." He then turned and exited the room without a word.

When the gentleman closed the door, Eve scrambled from the sofa to stand defiantly in front of Victoria. As she straightened her wrapper, she sneered, "You Englishmen are so weak. René would not have shied away from doing what must be done to a prisoner."

Victoria realized that the lady hadn't a clue to her identity and thought her a man. Suddenly remembering the long-ago lesson from Charles, she balled up her fist and planted Lady Frey a facer on her pert little nose.

The woman flew backwards across the sofa, then somersaulted completely off the furniture, landing on the floor. A trickle of blood appeared on her upper lip.

Shock and outrage evident on her face, Eve wailed, "You, sir, are no gentleman."

Victoria removed the wide-brimmed hat and grinned at the lady. "To be sure." She then gave a very feminine curtsy using the edges of her cape and left the stunned Lady Frey weeping on the floor.

With due speed she hurried downstairs to find Kit, fearful he would leave for Dover without her. But she discovered him in conversation with an older gentleman, who removed his hat upon her arrival. Unlike Lady Frey, he at once recognized Victoria as a female.

Kit, seeing his wife, said, "Victoria, allow me to present Mr. Grafton of Bow Street. My wife, Lady Ridgecrest."

The man gave Victoria a nod, then looked back at the viscount. "I'll take Lady Frey into custody. Do you wish me to summon my men to help you?"

"I can handle matters there." The fewer people involved, the less likely there was to be a scandal attached to his sister's name.

The runner nodded his head, tugged his hat at Victoria, then strolled up the walkway into Lady Frey's house as if he'd been invited to tea.

"I must go, my dear." Kit brushed a quick kiss on his lady, then turned and climbed into his curricle. As he picked up his reins, Victoria stepped into the carriage and settled beside him, a satisfied smile tipping her full mouth.

He stared at her, a frown marring his handsome face. "And where do you think you are going, my dear?"

"With you, of course."

Kit sighed and his gaze dropped to his wife's hands neatly folded in her lap, knowing he was about to have a protracted argument with the stubborn lady. He frowned, then reached over to pick up her hands. "Is that blood?"

"I do believe it is, but it is not mine."

Kit arched one brow as he stared at his wife in wonder.

"I fear it belongs to Lady Frey."

"Good God, do not tell me you drew her cork."

Victoria couldn't resist a contrite grin. "Leveled her with the ground."

Kit gave a hearty laugh, and shook his head. "Charles was right, your father should have given you a proper spanking. But I will say that you, my darling wife, are the most singular female it has ever been my delight to meet."

Then remembering the urgency of his mission, Kit set the curricle in motion, Victoria's horse trotting behind. "You may go with me, but promise you will not mill down anyone else."

"I promise." Victoria looked down at her hand. "In truth striking someone inflicts quite as much pain on the hand as it must on the nose being hit."

Kit laughed, then set his carriage in the direction of Dover.

White Lily Cottage was situated five miles northwest of Dover, some ways off the road from Canterbury. The journey from London had taken much of the

day, but Kit's need to rescue his sister drove him
onward despite fatigue. He'd been surprised that Victoria hadn't complained in the least, only encouraging him to spring his horses when he'd suggested she
remain behind at an inn where they'd changed teams
and left the trailing saddle horse behind.

The sun was lowering in the sky as they spied the
cottage sitting on a rocky knoll in the distance. It
was a charming two-storied stone building with ivy
growing up the granite walls and an abundance of
white lilies blooming in the surrounding garden.

Kit edged the curricle into the trees some ways
away. He surveyed the cottage with a practiced eye,
and wondered where Paul was. But there was no movement in or around the cottage. Kit didn't have the
time to search for his cousin. No doubt he would
show himself at the proper time.

Turning to Victoria, he took her by the shoulders.
"I shall get Isabel back, but if I have not returned by
dark, go to the inn we passed and summon the nearest
magistrate. Tell him everything about the Frenchman
and I'm certain he will bring armed men with him.
Do you understand?"

Victoria nodded, then threw her arms around Kit's
neck and kissed him hard. "Come back to me safe."

"I will, my love."

She watched as Kit made his way stealthily through
the trees. When the protective cover of the woods
was lost, he crouched low, following the stone wall
that surrounded the small garden to make his way to
near the open front gate. He knelt for a moment
eyeing the building, then slipped through the gate
to hide behind a large untrimmed boxwood.

Her heart leapt into her throat when a scruffy man
stepped from behind a large decorative stone and

aimed his pistol at Kit. She gazed in horror as a second man came from the front door of the cottage and signaled for Kit to come with them inside. Clearly they had been on the lookout.

Victoria jumped from the carriage, drawing her father's pistol from the pocket of her coat. She instinctively wanted to rush to save her beloved husband, then reason took hold. She would only get herself captured or worse, killed. Then what good would she be to Kit or Isabel?

He'd told her to go to the inn for help, but she was afraid that by the time she drove all the way back and summoned the magistrate, Kit might be dead and the marquis escaped.

Where the devil was Paul? If she could find him, perhaps they might have a chance to save Isabel and Kit. He had to be somewhere nearby, she thought, scanning the woods. She began to move slowly through the trees, cutting a wide arch around the cottage, never allowing herself to get close to the edge so that she could be seen from the windows.

Just as she came near the rear of the cottage the back door opened, and a young girl stepped out with a basket and began to walk straight at Victoria. The girl was sniffling and muttering to herself as she walked. She went to a small wooden building, barely shoulder high. With an angry yank, she pulled open the door. The sounds of startled cackling and squawking emanated from the structure.

As Victoria drew back to stay hidden, she felt the thump of the flask of laudanum in her cape and she was suddenly struck with an idea. The question was, could she get the girl to help or was she also a French spy?

The girl stooped, then disappeared into the hen-house and the noise of the disturbed hens grew louder. Within a matter of minutes she came back out, brushing feathers from her hair as she juggled the basket filled with eggs.

The maid's eyes grew round as a pistol seemed to materialize from behind a nearby tree and she found herself looking at what appeared to be a young man who had a finger over his pursed lips in a gesture of silence. He then signaled her to step into the woods with him.

Victoria could tell the girl was frightened, so she gently asked, *"Parlez-vous anglais?"*

"I ain't no Frenchie, sir. Just work for the owner of White Lily Cottage, and the marquis who's let the place while Mrs. White be in Tunbridge Wells takin' the cure for her arthritis. I can't say she'd be likin' all the gentleman's strange doin's here, if she knew."

"What is your name?"

"Sadie."

"I mean you no harm, but I need information. Can you tell me how many people are in the house, Sadie?"

The young servant shook her head. "Don't rightly know. They won't let me upstairs, but I've been hearin' a female voice up there since I come."

Victoria could only hope that Isabel had been locked in a room and left on her own unharmed. "What about downstairs?"

"Three Frenchies and an Englishman what just come, but I don't think he's happy to be here."

There was a great deal of risk in the plan that Victoria had, but she knew she had to try. "Sadie, how would you like to do a service for your country?"

The girl glanced back over her shoulder to the

house. "Are them Frenchies spies for Old Boney, sir?"

"Yes. Are you willing to help me?" Victoria held her breath, for the girl looked too young for such a heavy task, with thin blond curls hanging from under her cap to frame an innocent freckled face.

"Tell me what I must do." Sadie eyed the young man, thinking him rather too pretty for her taste, but if a frail lad like that could take the bit between his teeth and face down a bunch of Frenchie spies, then Sadie would too.

Victoria drew the flask from her pocket and handed it to the girl. "Can you put a good dose of this into whatever the Frenchmen are drinking?"

"Won't kill 'em will it?" Sadie took the bottle and sniffed it cautiously.

" 'Tis but laudanum. After they are asleep, give me a signal and I'll come in and free the lady." Once Isabel was free and safely away, Victoria could use her weapon to help Kit escape.

Just then the rear door opened and one of the men who'd taken Kit prisoner stuck his head out. *"Anglaise* wench, where ees our food?"

Sadie tucked the flask into her apron and stepped out from behind the tree. "I'm coming, sir."

Victoria prayed all would go as she'd planned.

Ropes cut into Kit's wrist as he shifted on the straight-backed chair where he'd been shoved after being bound. He'd been brought into the front parlor of the cottage, which was sparsely furnished with old-fashioned furniture, where the Marquis de Athier had been waiting for his arrival.

The Frenchman sat at a small table, a dueling pistol

in front of him while his men loitered in the front hall with pistols tucked in their coats. Kit hoped that Victoria was on her way to the inn to get help. The local magistrate might be the only thing that could save them now.

"*Monsieur,* we will not play the games, *hein?* I have your sister *and* her cousin, who foolishly tried to rescue the *mademoiselle,* locked in a room upstairs. You will tell me everything you know about Lord Carew's operation and all who work for him. But first, what became of my Evette?" The marquis gazed at him with malice.

Kit mentally cursed to know that Paul was a prisoner as well. Everything depended on Victoria getting to a magistrate. Seeing the marquis waiting expectantly for an answer to his question, Kit realized the truth about Eve might be too dangerous. "I assume we speak of Lady Frey. Was I supposed to be with her? I fear that my cousin sent word of your abduction of my sister, so whatever plan you and Eve had for me, did not occur."

René fingered the pistol in front of him, watching the Englishman closely. This British agent might be telling the truth and Evette might be unharmed, but there was little likelihood that *le Fantôme Anglais* would leave her free to escape. The Frenchman knew a moment of regret at the possibility she'd been caught. But his little Evette was resourceful and perhaps would escape on her own. No matter, it would be too dangerous to return to London to bring her safely to his yacht. It was unfortunate. She'd been very good at gathering information, but her usefulness to him and Bonaparte was now at an end. He would sail for France tonight and be in Paris in two days' time to reap the rewards of his long years in England. Before he left, he had this one last agent to deal with.

Matters had worked out quite nicely. His yacht could not again approach the shoreline until dark. Then they would take their prisoners on board and have much of the night, during their journey to France, to question this spy *vis-à-vis*. He knew they were safe since Evette would never betray his location even if she'd been captured.

So, he, René Anjou, had at last put an end to the English Phantom. There was much the man could tell him about the people in Portugal and Spain who aided the English as well as the partisans. With that knowledge the French might be able to totally crush the British network in the Peninsula. Once René knew all, Ridgecrest, his sister and cousin would easily disappear into the cold waters of the channel.

He rose, then looked at the men who'd come ashore the previous night from the *Mouette* to help him. In French he inquired, "Has that poor excuse of a maid finished preparing something edible for us to eat? Success makes me quite hungry."

The air grew cool as the sun sank lower in the western sky. Victoria peered around the tree where she sat hiding, to await the summons from Sadie, but she was beginning to doubt the young maid had been able to trick the Frenchmen into drinking the potion.

There was still no sign of Paul, which worried her. Was he sitting at the Black Knight Inn in Dover that he'd mentioned in his message or had he attempted to rescue Isabel before they'd arrived at the cottage? Victoria began to have a dreadful feeling that Isabel's cousin might be lying somewhere along the road from London, wounded.

Just then Sadie appeared at the rear door, motioning Victoria to come quickly. She scrambled down the sloping path, her heart pounding with fear.

Sadie whispered, "I was able to put laudanum in the servants' ale, but the marquis preferred wine from a bottle I weren't able to get my hand on. So he's still awake, but in the front parlour with the Englishman."

The maid had reduced the number from three to one, which greatly helped, but knowing the marquis was still in there unimpaired was frightening. "Is there a way I can get upstairs without the gentleman seeing me?"

The girl nodded, then signaled for Victoria to follow her. She entered the kitchen where the two Frenchmen lay with their heads propped on a table still cluttered with the remains of an unfinished meal. Soft snores emanated from the sleeping ruffians.

Wary that any slight sound might awaken them, Victoria slipped into the room on tiptoe. Sadie gestured to a narrow archway on the far side of the room. It proved to be a small flight of stairs.

Victoria turned to Sadie. "I thank you for your help, but I think it best if you return to your home to be safe."

Sadie nodded and needed no further urging. She hurried for the rear door and was gone within minutes.

Victoria took a deep breath and looked up the narrow stairwell, praying there was no guard with Isabel. Several of the old wooden steps creaked loudly as she climbed them, but there was no shout of alarm from above or below. When she reached the landing, she discovered there were but three doors off the small hallway. A key protruding from the lock in the nearest door on the left caught her eye. She was certain that was where Isabel had been put.

No noise drifted up from the front parlour, so Victoria tiptoed to the door, then turned the key which made a soft click. She entered the small bedchamber, closing the door behind her. Turning around, she halted in amazement.

Isabel Harden and her cousin Paul were seated on the edge of a four-poster bed. The young miss's head lay on the gentleman's broad shoulder and he clasped the lady around her waist with his right arm, his left hung limply at his side and was bound with strips of white muslin, now bloody from his wound.

Upon spying her sister-in-law, Isabel jumped to her feet but never left Mr. Harden's side. "Victoria!"

Victoria put her finger over her lip, signaling her sister-in-law to be quiet.

Miss Harden nodded her head, and in a quieter tone continued, "How glad I am to see you. We must summon a doctor at once, for that dreadful marquis has shot my dear Oak who bravely came to my rescue. 'Tis the strangest thing, but de Athier thinks Kit is some kind of spy."

A look passed between Victoria and Paul before he smiled and took Isabel's hand, bringing it to his lips. "Have I not told you it is but a scratch, my darling brat?" The gentleman, never taking his gaze off Miss Harden, inquired of Victoria, "Where is Kit?"

Victoria watched as the couple gazed at one another like a pair of moonstruck calves. Bemused she uttered, "Downstairs. The marquis has taken him prisoner."

Her statement seemed to snap them all back to the present. Paul rose and came to Victoria. "How did you get in?"

She quickly explained about Sadie and the potion. Paul listened, then said, "Good there is only one left. I think even wounded I can handle that scaly French scoundrel."

Isabel threw herself on his chest. "You mustn't, my love."

Paul kissed her upturned face. "Now, don't be getting all in a pucker, dear girl. I won't do anything foolish." He looked back at Victoria. "Have you a weapon, my lady?"

Just as Victoria pulled the pistol from her coat, the sounds of a carriage arriving at the cottage could be heard. Still holding the gun, she hurried to the window, but could see nothing, for the portal faced the rear garden.

When she turned back to look at Paul she could see worry etched into the lines on his face. Clearly they both feared that the visitors were more French come to aid the marquis. He reached out his hand for the gun, saying, "Take Isabel and escape out the back. Go for help—"

An unintelligible shout rang out, then the report of two shots echoed up the stairway to the room where the three stood. Victoria's face blanched white. With little thought except to get to Kit, she dashed for the door, but Paul was there before her. He took the pistol, ordering her and Isabel to wait in the room until he ascertained what had occurred. Victoria would have none of it. She had to get to her beloved Kit at once.

When Paul opened the door, she followed close behind. They tore down the front stairs, heedless of the danger. The first sight that greeted Victoria's eyes was Kit standing hale and hearty. Mr. Grafton was untying his hands. Then her gaze trailed lower to see the marquis lying unconscious on the floor of the parlour with a bullet hole in his chest. She returned her gaze to her husband, and he smiled reassuringly at her.

A wave of relief washed over her. Kit had come through the ordeal unscathed. She edged around Paul and practically flew across the room before throwing herself into her husband's freed arms.

Kit crushed his wife to him. He'd begun to think he might never see her beautiful face again as de Athier had begun to explain his plan to take Kit and Isabel to France.

Victoria turned her face up to his and he could see tears of happiness shimmering in her green eyes. He kissed her, heedless of the other occupants of the room, then grinned, knowing that the last obstacle to his surrendering completely to his wife's love lay wounded on the floor.

Remembering his duty, he thanked the Bow Street Runner for his rescue. Kit spied an older white-haired gentleman standing at the open door of the cottage watching them intently. Then he realized it must be the magistrate Victoria had summoned. Looking back to the runner to whom he owed his life, he said, "I'm grateful that you ignored my wishes, Mr. Grafton."

The man in the red vest grinned. "Lord Carew thought it best that you have some assistance, my lord. Wasn't my place to override your wishes, sir."

Glancing at Paul and Isabel, Kit realized that his cousin was standing with his arm around Isabel in a most improper manner. But how could he chastise him when the man had risked his life to save her. "Are you both unharmed?"

"Paul needs a doctor. He is gravely injured," Isabel said dramatically.

Paul lifted his injured arm. " 'Tis but a scratch." He then gave a slight bow to the old gentleman in the doorway. "Good evening, Your Grace. I'm surprised to see you involved in this matter. Thought you still in York."

Kit froze, realizing he was getting his first glance at his grandfather, the Duke of Townsend. He knew there should be anger and outrage for the years his family was ignored, but he was more than curious as to how the old gentleman came to be there.

His Grace stepped into the cottage, drawing off his York tan gloves. He gazed imperiously at the arm Paul had draped around Isabel. "I've been involved from the start, dear boy, and kindly cease handling my granddaughter in that vulgar manner." When Paul sheepishly removed his arm, the duke's gaze shifted to his grandson, a softening settling in their brown depths. "I was the one who recommended you, Christopher, to the Duke of York for a position with Lord Carew four years ago. The earl has kept me fully informed from the beginning."

Kit's brows drew together, his tone became angry. "I thought you had made it clear that you cared little what happened to my family."

The dark eyes under beetling white brows seemed to fill with pain. He shook his head, then gruffly announced, "Don't remind me of my youthful tyranny, dear boy. I've spent the last thirty years alone because my pride wouldn't let me admit that I was wrong about your mother . . . about everything. But I've followed you and your sister's lives closely. I guess I always hoped that you or Isabel might come to me one day to heal the breach I caused. But you both have your father's tenacity for making do on your own. I can only say you have made me proud." He looked from one grandchild to the other.

Kit was stunned. He'd always assumed the old man had never given them a second thought. To find that he'd been keeping a distant eye on them was humbling to say the least. Still, the person who'd been most affected by the duke's tyranny as he'd called it, was Kit's mother. "Sir, for myself I can say, I have no wish to continue the animosity, but 'tis my mother who has suffered the most because of your disapproval. She is the one with whom you must reconcile."

"And so I have, Christopher. I was in Grosvenor Square giving my heartfelt apologies to the lady and inviting her and my granddaughter to come to Townley House for the remainder of the Season when Lord Carew summoned me to your aid." The duke turned to look at his granddaughter. "Told her you need a proper come out ball, my dear. Gave her free rein to handle the entire matter. Spare no expense, I said. She has graciously accepted my offer."

Isabel, who been staring at her grandfather with awe, came hesitantly towards the duke, then straightened a bit defiantly. "You are too kind, Your Grace, but would you object to it being an engagement ball. I am quite determined to marry Mr. Harden."

The Duke of Townsend's gaze seemed to take in every aspect of his granddaughter's countenance. "I haven't the least objection to Mr. Harden's suit, but can you not bring yourself to call me Grandfather?"

The young lady threw her arms around the old gentleman's neck and she cried, "I should be delighted, Grandfather."

The duke looked over Isabel's shoulder at Kit, the old eyes shimmering with unshed tears. He then reached out his hand to his grandson and Kit stepped forward to embrace his grandparent and sister. Victoria found herself moved to tears as well by the reunion.

The marquis groaned on the floor, reminding all of the reason they were in the small country cottage. Kit suggested the ladies remove to the outdoors while the gentlemen took the prisoners in hand. Mr. Grafton quickly took command and had the wounded man taken to a carriage and his two sleeping companions bound. Within half an hour, Grafton and the men who'd accompanied him from London set out for Dover's gaol to house the prisoners till morning and tend to the marquis's wound. As the runner informed Kit, there was no cheating the hangman.

Victoria settled into a chair in the small parlour, watching Kit and his grandfather in deep conversation. She was too tired to even wonder about the nature of the discussion, all she could do was admire her husband's handsome countenance and revel in the knowledge that his dangerous assignment as a spy was ended at last.

When all was settled, the duke took Isabel and Paul in his carriage to the local inn to arrange a meal and accommodations for the night, leaving Kit and Victoria to close up at White Lily Cottage and follow.

As the other's carriage drew away, Kit turned to his wife and took her in his arms. "It has been quite an adventure, my love."

"So it has. More adventure than one might wish for, but I was never more amazed in my life than when we discovered the duke was involved."

Kit nodded, then grinned. "I have something else which will amaze you. Grandfather wishes me to take over the management of his racing stables. What say you to eventually living at Harden Castle in York?"

"Eventually?"

He leaned forward, his voice dropping to a low whisper. "Definitely eventually, but not yet." He began to nuzzle her ear.

Victoria's knees felt weak, a shiver of delicious anticipation running through her at the feel of his lips on her skin. "Then we are to join them at Townley House in London?"

Kit began to trace a line of kisses along the slender column of her neck, before raising his head. "We are leaving my sister and mother to my grandfather's care now that they are at peace. I am taking my bride on a honeymoon trip to Gracehill Castle in Scotland, which His Grace has graciously offered to us. There shall be only you and I for a long," he kissed her forehead, "undisturbed," he kissed her nose, "month," he kissed her mouth.

Victoria eagerly responded to Kit's kiss as her body melted against his. When at last he drew away, she was breathless.

"I love you my dear, beautiful Victoria. Shall we live in a castle in Yorkshire or return to Harwick?"

Victoria smiled dreamily up at him. "I love you, dearest husband. I would willingly live with you in the humblest cottage."

Kit grinned and looked back at the lit windows of the small stone house behind them. "Well, it isn't the humblest, dear wife. But it is quite ours to do with as we will for the remainder of the evening."

When Victoria gave a shy nod of her head, Kit swept his bride off her feet, and carried her upstairs. There were no thoughts of Frenchmen, or relatives or fortunes in White Lily Cottage that night. The English Phantom was at last able to take possession of his bride with tender passion and not a single distraction.

ABOUT THE AUTHOR

Lynn Collum lives with her family in DeLand, FL, and is the author of two previous Zebra Regency romances: *A Game of Chance* and *Elizabeth and the Major*. She is currently working on her next Zebra Regency romance, *Lady Miranda's Masquerade*, which will be published in June, 1999. Lynn loves hearing from her readers and you may write to her c/o Zebra Books. Please include a self-addressed stamped envelope if you wish a response.